# ONE MORE DAY

## STRIKEFORCE: BOOK TWO

# COLLEEN VANDERLINDEN

One More Day
Colleen Vanderlinden

Published in the United States
by Peitho Press

ISBN 1523707593

ISBN-13 978-1523707591


http://www.colleenvanderlinden.com

# DEDICATION

*Dedicated to my own personal
super team of beta readers and crusaders.*

*You guys are the absolute best..*

# CONTENTS

DEDICATION ..................................................................... iii

CONTENTS ......................................................................... v

CHAPTER ONE ..................................................................... 1

CHAPTER TWO .................................................................... 19

CHAPTER THREE ................................................................. 37

CHAPTER FOUR ................................................................... 54

CHAPTER FIVE .................................................................... 65

CHAPTER SIX ..................................................................... 89

CHAPTER SEVEN ................................................................ 104

CHAPTER EIGHT ................................................................ 110

CHAPTER NINE .................................................................. 129

CHAPTER TEN ................................................................... 139

CHAPTER ELEVEN .............................................................. 148

CHAPTER TWELVE .............................................................. 153

CHAPTER THIRTEEN ........................................................... 159

CHAPTER FOURTEEN .......................................................... 164

CHAPTER FIFTEEN ............................................................. 171

CHAPTER SIXTEEN ............................................................. 179

CHAPTER SEVENTEEN ......................................................... 192

CHAPTER EIGHTEEN ........................................................... 197

CHAPTER NINTEEN ............................................................. 203

CHAPTER TWENTY .............................................................. 215

EPILOGUE ....................................................................... 220

LETTER FROM THE AUTHOR .................................................. 223

ABOUT THE AUTHOR .......................................................... 225

# Part One
# Shadows

# CHAPTER ONE

"On your right," Caine's voice said over the comm in my ear. "He's about to let loose again."

"Copy." I swerved, turning back to the right and finally catching sight of the most recent powered dumbass Caine and I had been chasing. This one had been popping up all over the region the past two weeks, damaging buildings and injuring people in Chicago, Milwaukee, and Indianapolis, and then boasting about it on social media. If I had to guess, I'd say he was in his early twenties, probably. Tall and skinny, jock-looking type. He didn't bother with a uniform or costume of any kind, unless you counted black skinny jeans and a 1980s-era studded black leather jacket. He could fly, and he was able to breathe fire.

He called himself, predictably enough, "The Dragon."

Asshole.

Caine and I had spent most of a day trying to chase him down the last time he'd shown up in Detroit, with the rest of the team backing us up. He shouldn't have been as difficult to catch as he was, except that in addition to the flying and fire, he had the ability to camouflage himself. If you were anywhere where there were buildings or trees or anything like that for him to blend into, you were screwed.

Over the past hour or so, we'd managed to draw him out near the river and toward Belle Isle. It was more open there, and there were no skyscrapers for him to blend into.

I got ready to move, and the phone I kept in one of the pockets on my belt rang. Again. I rolled my eyes. This was the fifth time in maybe ten minutes.

"Shouldn't you answer that?" Caine asked as I hoisted him up and started flying toward the island.

"Not right now."

"What if it's your mom or something?"

I shook my head. "That's not her ring. It's Killjoy's."

Killjoy. Who I hadn't heard a peep from in over a month, since the day he'd come to visit me in the hospital wing after my fight with Maddoc. I'd told him to stay away from Command, because I didn't trust Alpha not to try to take him in. But that wasn't an issue anymore and if he'd bothered calling or messaging or something even once in all that time, he would have known that.

I dropped Caine on the beach at Belle Isle, where he could get a good shot off if I wasn't able to take the guy down. He wasn't getting away from us again.

"Ready?" I asked him.

"Go get him," he answered, pulling the stun rifle off his shoulder and aiming it. "If he starts taking off again, he won't get far."

I nodded, then rose into the air again. I knew by now, about a month after Portia had assigned Caine as my partner out in the field, that when he took a shot, he didn't miss. The problem was that we didn't get as many shots as we'd like, and superpowers, unfortunately, sometimes reacted strangely with the stun gun, so we had to make sure that we were somewhere where the chance of civilians getting hurt was low.

I also knew, because he'd told me the second we got our partner assignments, that his real name, secret identity or whatever you wanted to call it, was Ryan Lucas. To me, he was still Caine.

Superhero life. It's complicated.

I raced toward Dragon, who hadn't spotted us yet and seemed to be surveying the area below. Either looking for us or deciding which random structure to set fire to next. It really didn't matter, because he wouldn't get the chance to do any of it. Everything was a blur as I pushed myself toward him. His back was to me, and I had the perfect chance to get the jump on him, take him down before he even saw me coming.

And, at that moment, my phone rang again. Killjoy's ring.

Dragon spun and kind of did this funny mid-air version of tripping in surprise. I was already going at him full speed, so I just kept going, and I was lucky that he wasn't exactly a quick thinker. I barreled into him, got an arm around his neck, and flew with him back down to the ground. Even if he managed to take in enough air to blow fire, there was nothing on the beach to set fire to. I landed, and he struggled and fought against me. I could see Caine further down the beach, running toward us. Dragon kept struggling and trying to get out of my grasp, and I tightened my hold around his neck, his head under my arm.

And my phone rang again.

"Oh, for fuck's sake," I muttered. I used my free hand to dig my phone out of my belt pocket and answered.

"Hello?" I asked, well aware that I sounded like a bitch.

"Well hello to you too. I was wondering if you were ever going to bother answering," Connor's voice said over the line. Dragon started struggling again, and I yanked him back toward me.

"Little busy just now," I said.

"Yeah. Busy with Caine, huh?"

"What?"

"You two are always together. I see it on the news."

I was seriously tempted to throw my phone into the river. "I'm working. I literally have an asshole in custody right now and he's trying to get out of my grip and you're giving me bullshit about my patrol partner? Are you kidding me with this right now?"

"I— " he began, but now I was on a roll.

"And what business do you even have saying anything about anything? I haven't heard from you in over a month and I would have been sure you were dead except that I keep seeing you on the news."

"You told me to stay away."

"Oh kiss my ass," I gave Dragon a hard yank when he tried to get free again. "That has nothing to do with dialing the damn phone once in a while."

Caine met up with me and started putting the dampener over Dragon's neck while I held him still.

"So you're not going to say anything about Caine then?" he asked, and I held my phone away from my head and glared at it. Caine raised his eyebrows at me, oblivious to what was going on, and I shook my head.

"You can call back when you decide to stop being an asshole. I have things to do." I hung up and shoved the phone back in my pocket just as Caine activated the dampener.

"Everything okay?" Caine asked.

"Fine."

"Don't know who that was, but it seems like pissing off the chick who breaks buildings for fun isn't the brightest idea."

I shook my head. "Two buildings, man. Two. You act like I do that shit all the time."

We started walking up the beach, and I was more than happy to let Caine take over keeping a hold on Dragon. He smelled strongly of burnt eggs and I had to try not breathing through my nose or I'd end up losing my morning coffee in my mask.

"You forgot about that house in Brightmoor," he said.

"That didn't count. It was going to come down any day anyway."

"Uh huh. The Historical Museum?" he asked, glancing over at me.

"I didn't break the building. Just some of the stuff inside," I said with a grimace.

"Have they lifted the ban on you yet?"

I glared at him then, and he laughed and hauled Dragon into the mini jet we'd taken out for patrolling.

"You owe me lunch, by the way. I bagged this one," I told Caine as I buckled into the seat behind the pilot's seat.

"It's kind of unfair working with you. You end up bagging all of them."

"Yeah. All three of the ones we've managed to take down," I said, rolling my eyes.

Caine strapped Dragon into the seat beside mine, securing his hands and ankles and double-checking the dampener before sliding into the pilot's seat. Then he turned and looked back at me. "Hey. Better than leaving those three out on the street. We'll take a win where we can get it, and eventually, we'll start getting more of them. Right?"

I studied him for a moment. Dark mask covering everything but his mouth, he sported the same gray and black uniform I did. He looked a lot more menacing in his than I did in mine, though. "Who would have guessed you'd be the perky positive one of the two of us?" I asked him.

"Perky. Damn. You didn't have to get mean about it," he muttered, but I could tell from his tone that he was smiling. We took off, and I watched the city pass beneath us. I would have rather been flying outside of the mini jet than inside it, any day.

Within minutes, Caine was landing the mini jet at the flight bay at Command. We got out, and Caine talked to the flight crew about something with the jet while I hauled Dragon out of the plane. We took him down to the detention facility, handed him off gratefully to Marie and her people, then went up to Portia's office to fill her in on everything. By now, we didn't need to talk about how or when we were going to do something, or who would talk when, or what had to happen next. I'd been unsure about Caine as my patrol partner, and actually went as far as arguing with Portia about it because I would have preferred Jenson, but I had to admit that we worked well together.

It wasn't the same for everyone she'd paired up. Toxxin and Chance pretty much despised one another by now. Amy, AKA Steel, was kind of creeped out by Jenson and her self-replicating powers; and Monica thought Beta was, in her own often-repeated words, "an insufferable little know it all shit." Dani was intimidated by being paired with Portia because she was our leader, and she was constantly looking for someone to take her shifts for her.

So, yeah. Things were going really super well. For the most part, Caine and I were the only ones who managed to actually bring anyone in when they caused trouble, and even that wasn't all that often.

But, we were working on it. Portia had her hands full trying to keep all of us on task, and I didn't envy her the job.

We were heading for the elevator after dropping Dragon off when my phone rang again. This time it was Mama's ring, and I gestured for Caine to go ahead without me while I picked it up.

"Hey! What's up?" I asked, pacing back and forth near the elevators in the lobby between the men's and women's detention wings. I turned and paced back toward the men's wing. Through the window in the entry door, I could just see the cell at the end, and make out Maddoc's hulking form. I turned back around and put a hand to my neck, hating the way I felt on the verge of panic just from seeing him. The nightmares still hadn't stopped, and my reflexes and fine motor skills were still shot. Dr. Ali said it was likely I'd never be what I'd been. I still couldn't hit worth shit, and that had kind of been my thing. All I managed now was barreling into things at high speed. It got the job done, sometimes, but it wasn't pretty.

I shook my head, forcing the thoughts away and concentrating on Mama.

"Are you busy? I can call back," Mama said, and I smiled.

"Nope."

"I was wondering… I feel like a terrible person for even asking this but nothing else seems to work, and— "

"What is it?"

"You know those guys who moved in next to me? In Patty's old trailer?"

"Yeah. The bikers?"

"Yes. They've been really loud, and we've been calling the management on them, but they won't do anything. And Shelli even called the police twice, and they came but as soon as they were gone, it just started up again. They were shooting guns off out there last night."

I took a breath. "We have to get you out of there, Mama," I said, thinking of the house keys I had in my suite at Command. I'd just closed on a house I'd bought for Mama a couple of days ago, and I had some contractors coming to take a look at fixing it up so I could move her in. I hadn't told her yet, because I wanted it to be a surprise. And also because I didn't want her to argue with me.

"Not right now, Jo. And it's not just me. We have kids in this neighborhood."

"I know."

"I know it's not a StrikeForce thing. They're not powered or anything like that," she added quickly. "But do you think someone could come by and maybe talk to them? Maybe Beta?" She'd met Beta back when I was in the hospital and she'd taken a liking to him.

"Why not me?"

"I don't know how intimidated they'd be by a female superhero," she said.

"Mama. I have a reputation, you know."

"I know. But you know how some men are," she said, and she didn't have to explain, because, yeah, I did know. There was a type, and that type usually believed that anything a woman accomplished was actually thanks to someone else, that there was no way a woman, even a powered one, could beat up a big, strong man. Or, let's be honest, even a weak-assed one. They were the ones who suggested loudly and often on social media that my fights were all staged, that the villains I took in were actors, that Caine actually did all the work and I just swooped in at the end to look good. And you don't have to be a costumed superhero to get that shit. All you have to be is a woman who does things.

"Are they around now?"

"Yes. Neither of them seem to work or anything," she said.

"Okay. Sit tight."

"Is Beta coming?"

I sighed. "Mama."

"All right. Just be careful."

"Okay. Stay in the trailer, all right?"

"Love you, Ladybug."

"Love you more. Are you planning to make some of those double chocolate cookies of yours?"

"I am now," she said with a laugh. "I'll have them ready when you come to visit on Saturday."

"Yes!" I said, and she laughed again. "Okay. On my way."

I pressed my comm twice, which would get me Jenson instead of Caine. "Hey," I said.

"Congratulations on not breaking anything today," Jenson's cool, deadpan voice said in my ear.

"You all are really funny, you know that?" I asked, and I heard her laugh. "I'm just letting you know that I'm stepping out for a bit. My comm is still on but there's something I need to take care of." I thought for a second.

"Oh, and if there are any rumors about me roughing up some biker assholes later, they're totally made up."

I was pretty sure I heard a sigh on her end, but all she said was. "Duly noted, Daystar. See you at dinner."

I grinned and made my way up to the flight bay, then took off toward Warren, which was where Mama still lived and where I'd lived up until a few months ago, in the little yellow and white single wide in the Eight Mile Motor Village.

I landed on the cracked asphalt in the center of Perdition Lane. I could see Mama's trailer at the end. The flowers she had planted had long since died back from frost, and a light layer of new snow covered everything. The trailer next to hers was an old aqua and white monstrosity that should have been scrapped years ago. The tiny lot around it was strewn with old tires, beer cans and bottles, and empty pizza boxes, and there were three bikes parked there, three long-haired, tattooed guys standing around them. You know the bikers you see on the covers of certain romance novels? Mama loves those books. Anyway, these guys didn't look like that. Stringy, scrawny, oily looking, but clearly they think they're something special. I walked past my old neighbor and friend Robbie, who was fixing a car in his driveway with one of his buddies. I heard one of them murmur "oh, shit," and smiled behind my mask. I walked closer to the biker guys and they finally looked my way.

"There's no costume party around here, honey," one of the bikers said, and the other two immediately laughed. Dipshit hierarchy is so easy to peg. That one was the alpha moron, and the other two were his lackeys.

"I received a report that you guys were shooting guns here last night," I said, keeping my voice low. I crossed my arms over my chest and watched them. They couldn't see my face at all behind my mask, but I still tried not to look at Mama's trailer. I could hear doors opening as some of the other neighbors checked out what was going on.

"There's none of that powered shit going on here. You have no right to be here," alpha moron said.

I walked closer to them, arms still crossed over my chest, like I was taking a slow, casual stroll.

"If people feel unsafe, for any reason, I have every right to be here. And you are a problem."

Alpha moron held his hands out in a "come get me" gesture. "You think I'm scared of some bitch in a mask? You got any whips on you? We can make this fun if you like that kinky shit."

"I just threw up in my mouth a little bit," I said, and I heard a few quiet laughs behind me. "If you fire those guns again, I'm going to come back here and fucking feed them to you. And if you don't think I will, feel free to try me."

"You can't just come in here and threaten me. I have rights!" alpha moron shouted. Ugh. It's ridiculous how often we hear that one. It's like there's a pre-written script or something with some of these guys.

"And the people in this neighborhood have the right not to listen to your noise and see your garbage all over the place all the time. I'm done talking. I'll hear about it if you assholes don't calm down, and I promise you, I will be back. Enough with the loud music, the fighting, the shooting, and the breaking shit."

"Yeah, I'll break something, all right," alpha moron said, and he started coming toward me.

I heaved an exaggerated sigh. Even with my shitty reflexes, I could see his punch coming from about a mile away. He swung at me, and I grabbed his fist and wrenched it down then pulled his arm hard behind his back, twisting it just to the point where he felt like I was about to rip it out of its socket.

Self defense classes. Best hundred bucks I've ever spent.

I stood and held his hand behind his back as he shouted at me and called me things I knew Mama would want to hit him in the face with a cast iron frying pan for. The first of his lackeys got brave and took a swing at me and I grabbed his hand in mid-air and squeezed. I could feel the bones in his hand shifting in my grasp, and he screamed.

"Oh. Is that bothering you? Should I stop?" I asked innocently. The alpha moron kept saying rude things to me, and the lackey tried to kick my shin, and I put a little more pressure on both of them.

"Get her, dumbass," alpha moron said to the third lackey, who came toward me uncertainly.

"Don't piss me off, man," I said, and he glanced at his two pals again and backed away.

"Are you going to calm down or should I make it a little worse?" I asked the other two. I pulled alpha moron's arm back a little more, and he shouted.

"Okay, okay you crazy bitch. You're gonna rip my arm off!"

I let them both go, and they stood there for a minute, each of them massaging their injuries.

"I'm gonna sue your ass," alpha moron said.

I laughed. "Yeah, good luck with that."

"Now!" alpha moron said to the other one, and they both launched themselves at me.

I held my hands out, putting a hand over each of their faces and holding them back while they tried desperately to get at me.

"Okay," I muttered. I lowered my hands to the fronts of their shirts, grabbed the fabric in my fists, and then rose into the air.

I've found, in my short time as a super hero, that people don't like to be dangled from a few dozen feet up in the air. They start screaming, and then they start begging, and usually, there's peeing involved. And these two were the same way, but I was less than ten feet up into the air when the screaming started.

"So disappointing," I told them. I rose a little more. I was making a point here, after all.

When we were a good forty feet up, I stopped, letting them dangle, letting them get a good look at the asphalt below.

"So. Boys," I said. "Are you going to be good, quiet peaceful neighbors, or should I just drop you now and save everyone the trouble?"

"Yes!" alpha moron screamed.

"Yes, I should drop you?" I asked, acting like I was about to let him go.

"No! No, don't drop me. We'll be quiet. I swear we'll be quiet just put me down."

"What's the magic word?" I sang.

"You are fucking insane!" alpha moron screamed.

"Now. Was that nice? You could have hurt my feelings, if I had any." I started to open my hand a little, and he screamed.

"I'm sorry. Sorry. Please. Oh god please just put me back down. I swear."

"Very well." I came down for a landing and set them both down. Alpha moron puked at the side of the road and his buddy looked like he was about to do the same. "If I hear about you again, and I will, because I'm letting everyone here know right now that they can contact me anonymously via the StrikeForce hotline, and I'll come... if I hear about you again, I won't be nearly as nice. Do we understand each other?"

"Yes," alpha moron groaned, still hunched over on his hands and knees.

"Lovely." I glanced around at the neighbors who had assembled to watch the drama. "Have a nice day," I said, then I rose into the air. I had to grin when I heard applause erupt from below.

I was almost back to Command when Jenson contacted me via my comm. "Did you really have to do the whole dangling them in mid-air thing?" she asked.

"I have no idea what you're talking about."

"One of them called to complain."

"Hm."

"And seven of your mother's neighbors called to thank us for caring about them enough to send you."

"That was nice of them," I said. "Are we still binging on pizza and movies later?"

"I wouldn't miss it."


Two hours later, I was dressed in my grungy old sweats and t-shirt, heaping pizza and bread sticks from the dining hall onto a plastic tray. I surveyed the tray, then added more pizza. Jenson could put away more food than I'd ever seen anyone manage. I shoved the tray down the line until I got to the drink station, and I grabbed two cans of cream soda and tried to fit them onto the tray. I gave up and shoved one under each of my arms, then picked up the tray and headed for the elevators. I looked at the "up" button with some consternation, then lifted my leg to see if I could tap it with my foot. The second I did that, one of the cans of soda slid out from under my arm.

"Shit."

"Hold on," I heard Caine say, and I glanced behind me, where he was coming out of the gym. He bent and picked up the can, then hit the button for me.

"Thanks."

He nodded. We got onto the elevator and he hit the button for my floor. We rode in silence for a bit.

"So. Hungry?" he asked, looking at the tray while taking the other can of soda out from under my arm.

"It's not all for me," I said.

He raised his eyebrows.

"Have you ever seen Jenson eat? Most of this is hers. And she's in charge of getting the food next time," I muttered.

He didn't say anything for a second, and then he let out a low laugh. "So you beat up some bikers today?"

"I barely touched them," I told him. "It's amazing how they're all badass and stuff when faced with a bunch of older ladies and single moms, but you dangle them in the air a little bit and then they're puking at the side of the road. 'Please, please stop, oh God,'" I mimicked them in a high tone, and Caine laughed.

The elevator stopped at my floor and he walked me to my room, then took the tray while I put my thumb to the door lock. I pushed the door open and took the tray from him, and he followed me in and set the cans down on my little kitchen counter. I never cooked there. Why cook when there's a ready supply of anything I'd ever want to eat down in the dining hall?

"Thanks," I told him, and he nodded. "Um. I would invite you to stay, but we're watching Jane Austen movies and it's about to get girly in here. And Jenson has a reputation to uphold, you know."

He shook his head. "Nah, I'll leave you to it. Jenson's secret is safe with me," he said with a smirk.

"Don't be smug. I'll see you bright and early." He nodded, then let himself out of my suite.

I set the tray of food on the coffee table in the living room, then looked around for napkins since I'd forgotten to grab some from downstairs. As I looked, I contemplating calling Connor, since I had a number to get in touch with him at now, but I was still more than a little pissed over his attitude from earlier. Especially the jealous insinuations, let alone the whole disappearing from my life for over a month. And the stupid thing was, for an instant in the elevator with Caine, I had felt guilty. Not because there was anything even remotely happening there, but because Connor had planted it in my head, just in those few words on the phone, that spending any time with Caine was somehow wrong.

Screw that. The last thing I need is to start feeling guilty for things I haven't even done. There are enough real things I should feel guilty about.

Jenson showed up, interrupting my ragey thoughts, and we settled in to eat and watch movies. We were on to *Sense and Sensibility* when she nudged me with her elbow.

"What?"

"I was thinking."

"Oh, shit."

"Kiss my ass, Faraday," Jenson said, and I laughed. "I was thinking, and I mentioned it to Portia, that it might be fun for us to get together outside of work, outside of here. Like normal people."

"We're not normal."

"But we can pretend to be, just for a little while. And we thought that maybe we could do a girls' night out thing soon. Let Caine and David be on duty together one night so we can get the hell out of here for a bit."

I didn't answer.

"Don't be too thrilled. Try to restrain your excitement a little bit," she said, holding her hands up like she was trying to hold me back. Then she grabbed another slice of pizza and bit into it.

"What would we do?"

"Christ, Jolene. Have you ever just hung out with anyone?"

I looked at her, and she rolled her eyes. "Fine. We'd go out to eat. Maybe go catch a movie afterward or hit the casinos if we're feeling lucky. Just get out of here and the uniforms for a little while. And maybe get to know each other as people and not just co-workers. Maybe it would help some of the problems we're all having working together."

"I have no problem working with my partner," I pointed out.

"That's because Caine is the most laid-back person I've ever known, unless you give him a reason not to be. Anyone else would probably drive you nuts and then there would be threats and ugliness and then we'd have a mess."

"You know, I requested you as my partner," I told her.

"Aw. You do care. I wish Portia had gone for that. Amy's a great lawyer but she's not a good match with me."

"It's the multiple yous that freak her out," I said.

"Thanks."

We watched for a little while longer, and then she looked over at me. Then she grabbed the remote and turned it off.

"It was just getting to the good part," I told her.

She gave me a withering look.

"Rickman was about to get all dreamboaty," I told her, and she rolled her eyes. "You know men only love women like that in movies, though," I added, thinking back to Connor and his attitude.

"Focus, Jolene."

"What?"

"I had to freeze several of Alpha's accounts today," she said. "There was money being siphoned out of them that I never approved, and neither did Portia. You don't know anything about that, do you?"

I didn't answer, and that was pretty much all the answer Jenson needed.

"Why, Jolene?"

It had taken them longer to figure it out than I'd thought it would when I went to Luther about siphoning funds from some of Alpha's accounts. Not a lot. Just a little here and there, but nothing at all compared to the enormous amounts of money in the accounts. She'd set it up with one of her nieces, who was a genius at crap like that. We'd moved the money around and eventually deposited some into my accounts, and some into Luther's. Her fee.

"I hardly think he's gonna miss it," I told her.

"That's not the point. What, are you still robbing houses, too?"

"No."

"But you'll steal from StrikeForce."

"I'm not stealing from StrikeForce. I'm stealing from Alpha, and Alpha is definitely fucking not StrikeForce."

"You're splitting hairs," she said.

"I'm not planning to keep it."

She gave me a look that told me she wasn't buying it.

"I'm not."

"Giving it away to charity doesn't really count either. It's still stealing. And then there's the whole separate issue of wondering if you really think I'm that stupid, that I wouldn't notice thousands of dollars going missing every week."

"I don't think you're stupid. There are a lot of accounts there. I figured you or Portia would figure it out eventually, but I didn't think you'd trace it back to me so quickly."

"I didn't trace it back to you. It was a hunch," she said. She turned the movie back on.

"Jenson, what do you think is going to happen to the team once Alpha finally gets transferred to international custody?" The plan was to gather enough evidence to be able to turn him over to the international tribunal that dealt with powered people. There was the obvious, the way he'd kept several of us jailed and dampened to use as his own private army against our will, but Jenson was sure that some encrypted files she'd found after our takeover would prove that there was even more to the story, and David and Jenson were working on cracking them.

"Once he's in custody, we lose all of this," I said, gesturing around, indicating StrikeForce Command in general. "No building. No fancy mini jets. We lose access to all of the computers and communications systems in this place, let alone the joy of having people cook and clean for us all the time. What happens to StrikeForce then?"

"We'll figure it out."

"With no money, and nowhere to operate from, how long do you think this team will stay together? We're hanging on by a thread here as it is."

She kept looking at the screen. "So you were stealing from Alpha to try to support StrikeForce?" she asked dubiously.

"Yes. Don't be so surprised."

She turned the movie back on and we watched it in silence for a little while. "As a plan, it's not a terrible one. It's still stealing, though."

"Yeah."

She sighed. "It's finished now, though. And, I don't know, maybe trust me enough to tell me when you're doing something like that?"

"Would you have said 'yeah, Jolene, go ahead and embezzle money from Alpha. That's a great idea!' No. You wouldn't have."

"I might have, if you'd explained what you just told me," she argued. "Have a little damn faith in me. I backed up your plan to overthrow Alpha. I was with you every step of the way, and you still want to hide crap from me."

"We argue like a married couple," I muttered.

"No. We argue like friends who should actually give a damn about one another. I felt like an idiot when I realized what was happening, that you did it and didn't even think twice about me stumbling across it."

We fell into silence again. "I'm sorry. Okay?"

"Fine. Next time we do a movie night, you're grabbing Chinese food, though."

# CHAPTER TWO

The next morning, Caine and I made it through our patrol shift without much trouble, and then I spent the afternoon informing Luther (the little old Polish lady who was also the best fence and con woman I'd ever known) that our little game with Alpha's money was off. She wasn't entirely thrilled with me.

I was on my way back to Command, replaying a nightmare I'd had the night before, after Jenson had left, about my face-off against Maddoc. In the dream, I was back there again, struggling for my life, Maddoc's hands around my throat, his a mask of rage above me, and no matter how hard I struggled, hit, scratched, kicked... no matter what I did, none of it made a difference. Unlike what had actually happened, though, in the dream I wasn't able to use Toxxin to knock him out, and he just kept strangling me, until I felt my body give up on me. And when it was over, when I was gone and he'd left my body there, I was able to watch and see that life went on without me, as if I'd never been there at all and nobody noticed that I was gone.

I hadn't been able to fall back asleep afterward. I guessed maybe it was a guilty conscience thing after my talk with Jenson. Whatever it was, I didn't want to go through it again.

I was about to turn toward downtown when Jenson clicked onto my comm.

"Daystar, what's your location?"

"I'm near Wayne State. Why?"

"Can you go over by Campus Martius? We're getting calls about a disturbance over there and everyone else is already out on calls. It's like everyone decided to go nuts in one night."

"I'll head over there now."

I swerved toward the New Center area. Campus Martius Park eventually came into view, the ice skating rink lit up for evening skaters. Soon, the Christmas tree lighting would happen, and the whole park would be full of twinkling lights. For now though, things looked quiet and calm, and a few skaters took advantage of the ice and the cool weather. I was about to contact Jenson and tell her nothing was going on when I saw a dark shadow moving toward one of the side streets off of Woodward. I came in for a landing, ending up behind a parking garage. I didn't want to draw attention to myself. The second anyone noticed me, I'd be all over social media. I hated that shit.

I walked down the street, taking the same direction the dark shadow I'd noticed had taken. The pavement was slick and oily, and napkins and other debris from the nearby food places stuck to the concrete. The street lights flickered overhead, casting a blue-white glow onto the buildings and parking meters nearby. The only sounds were the roar of traffic from the street and the plinking sound of the heavy raindrops falling on metal awnings and trash dumpsters as icy rain began to fall. I searched for a good ten more minutes without seeing anything. I wasn't sure if I was relieved or annoyed.

I pressed my comm. "Daystar checking in. I'm going to do one more sweep of the area but so far things look okay here. Once I'm done, I'm going for a fly," I said, glancing up at the sky.

"In this weather?" Jenson asked over the comm, and I smiled.

"Are you going to ask me if I brought my umbrella?"

"Of course not. Your suit is waterproof."

"Well, there you go. Don't wait up. I need to clear my head," I said, flashing back to my nightmares about Maddoc and my lingering annoyance with Connor.

"Okay. Let me know if you need anything."

"I'm going silent now, okay?" I asked, knowing she'd worry.

I heard Jenson sigh over the comm. "Okay. Be careful," she said in a resigned tone.

"Aren't I always?" I asked in mock seriousness, and I heard her laugh before I turned off my comm. I didn't want anyone squawking in my ear. All I wanted was the sky and to feel like I was still the same old me. When I flew, I wasn't too slow. I wasn't clumsy. I wasn't less than I used to be, before Maddoc. No, when I flew, it was like everything was as it should be.

I finished checking the alley and was about to lift off when I saw something shift in the shadows. My body tensed, the immediate adrenaline that came with seeing something unknown in the dark rushing through me.

"Easy. I'm not here for an ass-kicking," the shape said as he stepped out of the shadows. I tried not to let on how my stomach flipped, how my face heated beneath my mask when I realized who it was, even though I was still kind of pissed at him. That rough voice, that hint of a Scottish brogue. Broad shoulders, a massive body clad head to toe in black.

"So, you're back," I said softly to Connor as he stepped further out of the shadows.

"For the moment," he said. "Did you miss me?"

I shrugged, relieved that he couldn't see my face. "Maybe."

"Maybe, huh?"

"Maybe," I repeated.

"You were good and pissed when I talked to you yesterday," he said.

"Well, that's because you were an asshole when I talked to you yesterday." I crossed my arms, and he stepped closer.

"Maybe I was."

"Hm."

He took another step toward me. "Since you're bein' a coy little thing, I'll say it: I missed you. Even if you are mad at me."

"I'm mad at you because you were talking stupid yesterday. And because as far as I knew, you forgot I even existed."

He reached out and put his hand on my hip and drew me closer to him. "It's impossible for me to forget that you exist. And as for talking stupid, all I can do is blame the fact that I missed you and I hated that he gets to spend every day with you and I can't."

"You could have come back to see me. Alpha isn't a problem anymore," I said softly, feeling myself melt a little bit.

"I know. I realized that soon after I visited you that day."

"Then why didn't you come back?"

He shrugged. "Something came up. And you were busy, as well."

"I'm not the only one," I said. "CNN's been all over you. They love it when you turn up somewhere."

He shook his head.

"That fight in Britain was something else," I said, looking up at him. "Six of those Wrecker assholes?"

He stepped a tiny bit closer to me, the fronts of his thighs coming into contact with my legs. "Pretty sure it was eight," he said.

"CNN said six."

"And how accurate are they, usually?" he asked, and I could hear the humor in his voice. "How many of your captures have they reported as being a team effort?"

"They were a team effort."

"Sure they were. You did all of the ass-kicking, and then your team comes in and cleans it up when you're done." There was something in his voice, the slightest hint of anger that made my spine tingle, just a little. "Well, yeah," I said. "Like I said, a team effort."

"You need to stop telling them to hang back. All of them."

I looked up at him in surprise. "How did you know I tell them that?"

"Because that's how you are. You'll take the hits to keep them safe, and you're too stubborn to listen when they argue with you."

"It has nothing to do with keeping them safe," I insisted, stepping back and crossing my arms.

"No?"

"No. I'm trying to get back in fighting form. I'm still too damn slow. All I can do is charge and hope I knock them out with the impact. Still can't punch worth a shit, and kicking is even more pathetic. And to do it the way I have to, I need room and to not have to worry that one of them is in the damn way."

He stepped close again, raised his hands to my shoulders. His fingers brushed against my neck and I flinched back, remembering, in that one brief touch, the feel of Maddoc's hands wrapped around my throat as I struggled to breathe, as my heart began to give out on me, as the world went black. I shivered, hating myself for being so stupidly weak.

"Sorry," he murmured. "I'm sorry." He rested his face against the top of my head.

"It's okay," I said. After a moment, I uncrossed my arms and leaned into him, resting my hands at his hips. "I do that every time someone touches my neck now. Jenson was trying to put this necklace my mom bought for me on, and I completely fucking freaked out," I said angrily.

He snaked his arms around my body and drew me close, and I held him as well. We must have been an interesting sight, him in his black body armor, me in my StrikeForce uniform, holding one another in the pouring rain.

"We should get out of the rain," he said.

I thought for a second, running through the options in my head. I still had the crappy apartment I'd rented after Mama not-so-gently nudged me out of her place. But it was risky flying over there and then trying to duck into my apartment in uniform like this. Anywhere else we went, we'd likely end up with our pic all over Twitter or something. Give the bloggers and livestreamers something to talk about, I thought with a grimace.

"We could go back to Command," I said. "I mean, now that Alpha's out, I'm not worried about him trying anything stupid."

He nodded. "Sounds good."

"We're not too far. Do you want me to fly you there?"

He shook his head. "I'll meet you there. Outside the main lobby?"

I nodded, and watched him recede into the night. He'd be there sooner than seemed possible. It was one of the many things he could do. Accelerated speed. Healing factor. Super strength. And the thing of it was, I wasn't even sure that was all of it. I shook my head and rose into the air, heading east toward where StrikeForce Command rose in the distance, a glittering group of steel towers along the river.

A couple of minutes later, I came in for a landing in the courtyard between the four towers that made up StrikeForce Command. The main tower stood in the center, flanked by the other three, slightly smaller towers. As I looked around, I saw Killjoy walking toward me. I'd beat him by maybe half a minute, I realized.

"What, did you stop for coffee or something? I was half-sure you'd beat me here somehow," I said, and he shrugged.

"Must be getting slow in my old age," he joked, and I shook my head. We walked toward the entrance to Command, and the two guards there greeted me, then gave me a quick scan. Killjoy had to sign in, and I had to sign for him, and then they scanned him as well. Our door guys don't play around. There was no slacking off, no just waving someone past. I kind of wanted them to stand outside of Mama's trailer and keep an eye on things, but I didn't think Portia would go for it.

We walked in and I waved at the new receptionist. She'd worked up on one of the administrative floors before, but now that Jenson was more involved with patrolling and other team duties, she had moved down here to take her place. Janice or Janet or something like that. I didn't have it committed to memory yet. I led Killjoy to the corridor that led from the main tower to the residence tower, then we took the elevator up to my floor. We passed the time wordlessly. I was a mix of nerves and lingering annoyance from the way he'd acted when he'd called me. Though I had to admit that some of that had been abated by how happy I was to finally see him again.

We got off the elevator, and then I led him into my suite. It was still pretty bare, though I did have some little knickknacks and other stuff around. No pictures of me and Mama, because I wasn't ready to take a chance yet. I mean, my teammates had all met her, but I still just didn't like the idea of mixing my actual life with my StrikeForce life.

I closed the door behind us, studying Killjoy as he looked around. The question was, what part of my life did he fit into? Did he bridge the gap between actual life and whatever this was I was doing with StrikeForce? Right now, I didn't have the foggiest idea, but I kind of hoped he was something more than just someone who took an interest because of the super hero thing.

"I'm going to go change real quick," I told him, plucking at my StrikeForce uniform. The gray and black body armor, full face mask, and boots did a great job of keeping me protected and incognito, but I didn't want that now that I finally had him there with me. In my bedroom, I peeled off my uniform and pulled on a pair of jeans and a top that wasn't too horribly wrinkled. I pulled my hair down and ruffled it a bit, letting my bangs fall over my face. It was funny how just that one stupid thing made me feel more like Jolene, and less like Daystar.

When I went back out into the living room, Connor was still standing there in his armor, his mask. He still seemed uncomfortable with the idea of me seeing his face. I understood, I guess. Our secret identity is the only part of our old lives that's still ours, and if he had family to protect, as I did, then I understood it even more.

I hoped, eventually, he'd trust me enough to take the mask off.

There was no reason for me to keep the mask on. He'd seen my face before I was Daystar, when I was a burglar, and we'd stayed in touch, on and off, ever since.

We stood awkwardly in the living room.

I glanced at him, then looked away. My suite felt even smaller with him in it.

"So," he began.

"So," I repeated.

He laughed. "I haven't been this fucking nervous around a woman since I was about fourteen."

"Why in the hell would you be nervous?" I asked incredulously.

"Oh, come on. You could kick my ass without even thinking about it. You're smart as hell and you've got your shit together. You're everything I'm not, sweetheart."

Well. He could call me 'sweetheart' any damn time he wanted. That low, growly voice.

I tried to remember why exactly I was mad at him again.

I pulled myself together. I hoped I looked calmer than I felt. One thing I promised myself, after seeing the way my mom was with my dad, the way she loved him, fawned over him, even after he started smacking her around…. I swore I'd never, ever be a fool for a man, and I could see, all too easily, becoming a fool for Connor, for a guy who hadn't even bothered to let me see his face yet.

"Everything you're not, huh?" I asked, settling onto the couch. He folded his bulky frame onto the chair across from me.

"Yeah."

We sat in silence for a while longer.

"You haven't nagged me about taking the mask off," he finally said.

"Were you timing me to see how long it would take?"

"Maybe."

I shrugged. "It's not like I don't understand the value of keeping secrets. I figured you'd take it off when you were ready. Or not," I added with another shrug.

He gestured to me, waved me over to him, and I stood up and crossed the few steps to where he was. He gently pulled my hand, and I lowered my body uncertainly until I was sitting across his lap.

"Go ahead," he said quietly.

"You don't have to. It's okay," I said.

"I want to. I want you to see me, Jolene."

I raised my hands to the bottom of his mask, all too aware, distracted by his hard body, his thighs under me, his broad chest, his gloved hands resting on the arms of the chair.

I slowly raised the bottom of the mask, first revealing the strong jaw I'd pictured way too often since that day he'd kissed me in my hospital room, that scruff of golden-red hair across his jaw and chin. Firm lips, the bottom one just full enough to make me want to take a nibble. I raised the mask up over his narrow nose, up to a pair of the most gorgeous, deep blue eyes I'd ever seen. His eyes were so vibrant it took me a moment to register the long, jagged scar that crossed from just above his right eye, down to the corner of the left side of his mouth. I took it in, and he stayed silent, still as a statue. I kept my eyes on his face as I pulled the mask the rest of the way off, revealing a head of short golden-red hair, trimmed close to his head.

I sat looking at him.

"Pretty bad, huh?" he asked.

"Oh, I don't know," I said. "I've seen uglier."

He laughed, and I laughed along with him. I lifted my hand to his face, gently traced the scar with my fingertips. It was rough, uneven, as if it had healed badly. How had this happened to someone with a healing factor?

"Want me to put the mask back on?" he joked.

"No," I said, pulling my fingertips back from his face, appalled by how mindless I was. What was I doing, touching him like that? "How did it happen? Why didn't it heal?"

He took a breath, and it seemed like he was trying to decide something or come to a conclusion about something. "It happened before I got my powers," he said. I just sat and watched him, waited for him to go on. He shook his head. "I didn't always do the superhero thing."

"That makes two of us."

"Yeah. I mean, I wasn't a good guy."

"Same. Burglar," I said, shrugging. "But you already knew that."

He took another breath, looked way from me. "I was worse."

I felt dread settle into my gut. "We don't have to do this now."

"Yeah, we kind of do."

"Why?"

"Because I want you, and I think you might, maybe want me, and I want you to know exactly what you're getting into here."

"Okay. How bad?"

"Before I got my powers, I did some illegal shit."

"More illegal than breaking into houses and banks?"

"Yeah."

I waited, and after a moment, he went on. "We talked before about how we understood each other, what it was to grow up with nothing."

I nodded.

"It's easy to turn to crime when you think you have nothing to lose. That's why I never judged you the way those costumed assholes do. I get it. They can tell us it's wrong all they want, but you did what you thought you had to do."

"I'm still doing it," I said quietly.

"What?"

"Stealing," I said, not wanting to meet his eyes.

"What? You're breaking into houses?"

I shook my head. "From Alpha."

He sat back. "Explain that."

"My... partner, fence, whatever... was helping me funnel some of Alpha's money into my own accounts. I've made a nice amount so far," I finished.

He didn't answer, and after a moment he shook his head. "I'm impressed. I don't feel sorry for Alpha."

"So yours is worse than being a superhero and still being a thief?"

"Yeah. I started as a thief, worked my way up, became known as a guy who could find things that nobody wanted found, sell it to you for the right price. I didn't care what it was, or who wanted it. Or who got hurt as a result."

"What did you find for people? What kinds of things?"

"Drugs, weapons, secrets... name it, I tracked it down and sold it. I was good at getting into places nobody wanted people to be. Good at keeping secrets and staying on the move. I made more money than I even knew what to do with. Hoarded it all." He paused. "People died because of the shit I sold, Jolene."

I nodded. "And this?" I asked, gesturing toward his scar.

"I sold a pretty nasty weapon to some guys who used it. Blew up a daycare to get back at one of the women whose kids went there. Some political bullshit."

"Jesus."

"One of the fathers... he lost his wife and his kids in the explosion... he tracked down one of the guys who did it. And before he killed him, he got my name out of him. Where to find me. The guy tracked me down, gave me this. I couldn't even fight him back. The grief on his face... nothing I could do to him could be wore than what I'd already done. So I ran."

I nodded. It was all coming together. "So you got powers in the first Confluence, and you decided to use them for good, to try to make up for some of the things you did before."

He shook his head. "You want to believe that, sweetheart. That wasn't who I was."

"So..."

"I became a super villain."

I laughed, sure he was messing with me, and he met my eyes. I froze at the look in his eyes. "What was your super villain name?" I asked, playing along, because this sure the hell couldn't be for real. Not him. A tiny voice taunted me, telling me that, in the end, I was just like my Mama when it came to men.

"Raider."

I did laugh then. "Raider's a chick," I said, rolling my eyes. I moved to stand up, and he caught my arm in his hand.

"Jolene."

"You're being stupid," I said.

"I was the first Raider. Look it up," he said, still holding on to me.

"Then who's she? And how'd she get the name?"

30

"She got the name because she was on my former team and they all thought I died in a fight," he said. Then he took a breath. "And also because I used to be married to her."

I shook him off then, and this time, he let me go. I stood up and walked over to the window. I wanted to believe that this was his weird sense of humor. This was the same guy who'd once tossed Maddoc out a window at me because he'd expected me to catch the villain. He had to be messing around.

Right?

The silence hung between us. I didn't know what to say, and he apparently seemed to think he'd said enough. I got up and walked over to the floor-to-ceiling windows, overlooking downtown. I looked out them for a while, then turned back to him.

"So," he said, looking up at me. "What has you more pissed? That I was a thief, a super villain, or that I was married to a super villain?"

"Who says I'm pissed?" I asked. I turned back to the window again.

"You have that look on your face, like you wouldn't mind hitting me hard right now."

I didn't answer.

"Aren't you glad now that I told you this before we did anything you couldn't come back from?" he asked. I heard him stand. I waited for the sound of his footsteps receding, the door opening and closing, but it didn't come. Eventually, I turned around to see him still standing there, arms crossed over his chest.

"If you were Raider... if you were anything like the current Raider, it means you killed people."

"Does it really matter?"

I didn't answer, and he kept his eyes on me.

"So...how did you get from there to here?" I asked him. Give me something, please, I silently pled. Convince me that the things I believed about you weren't all lies.

He sat down again. "They thought I died. There was a big fight, our team and a bunch of special ops type superheroes. They kicked my ass, shot me up pretty good, and I fell into the bay where we were fighting." He nodded. "I came to, after I healed enough of my injuries, in this big warehouse. They kept me alive, talked to me, told me shit about my team that I hadn't known."

"Like what? What, was your wife cheating with another of your teammates or something?"

"That bothers you more than you want to admit. Almost like you're jealous or something."

"Answer," I snarled.

"That they were making deals behind my back. All that time, I thought I was in charge. I never really was," he said. "I got to know them, and the better I got to know them, learned more about them, the more I wanted to be like them, to make sure I never made the same mistakes again. To make sure that I played the game by my own rules and put my trust in the right people."

I didn't answer for quite a while, and he seemed content to wait it out.

"I think maybe we should call it a night," I finally said.

"Is there anything you want to ask me?" he asked, standing up.

I shook my head.

"So... what does this mean for us?" he asked quietly.

I shook my head. "People don't change that much. And I've got plenty of my own crazy to deal with," I said. "And it seems to me, it's kind of odd that Raider and the rest of that team are all still out there, running around causing trouble, and no one's done anything to stop it. You'd think that somebody who knew them as well as you did would have easily been able to step in and stop them, if he wanted to." I met his eyes then, and he didn't look away.

"I'm working on it. Raider's second-in-command is is a precog. Every time I've decided to go after them, she knows, and they move before we can get to them."

"Well, that's a pretty worrisome power to be dealing with. Even more reason to catch them as soon as possible, huh?" I asked, walking past him toward the door. He reached out and gently pulled my arm, making me stop.

"You were never all in on this hero shit," he said, freezing me with the intensity of his gaze. "You're still not. When it comes right down to it, you're all about you, and that's fine."

I didn't answer.

"We're a lot alike, Jolene," he said, rubbing his thumb over my knuckles. "I told you this because I think we have something here worth building on. I want you in my life, working with me. By my side."

"I— "

"And you can try to shut me out now," he said. "But I'm not giving up. You'll remember, once you're over the shock of what I just told you, how well you and I understand each other. You'll remember that this StrikeForce shit was never what you wanted. And you'll be mine."

I pulled my hand out of his and stepped away. "See, now that? That right there? That sounds kind of asshole stalkery."

He rolled his eyes then pulled his mask back on. "You're completely over-reacting."

"Am I?" Stupid as it was, I wanted him to convince me. I wanted to forget what he'd told me. I wanted to go to him and pretend this conversation had never happened. I wanted him to kiss me again. I wanted to learn every contour of his jaw and neck, memorize the taste of his lips. I wanted it not to matter that he wasn't everything I'd thought he was, that he hadn't sounded more than a little stalkery just then.

But that wasn't me. Careful is the way I've stayed free. The few times I've acted stupidly were the only times I got caught, or even came close to getting caught. Nothing about getting involved with Connor was careful, or smart. "I'm glad you told me, though," I added.

He let out a short, angry laugh. "Yeah. I bet you are."

"Not…I'm glad you think enough of me to be honest with me. That means a lot," I told him.

"You think this is over," he said. "It's not."

"It's over when I say it's over, Connor."

He took a step toward me, and it took everything in me not to take a step back. "No. It's over when I say it's over. And that's pretty much never going to happen."

"I want you to leave now. Let's go."

He didn't respond for several long moments, then he nodded. "Okay. I have a thing I have to do tomorrow. I'll probably be gone for a little while again. Which is probably good. It'll give you time to think and process all of this."

"I need to know something."

"What?"

"You're not doing the super villain thing anymore. Right?"

"Of course not. I see how small and stupid I was before. I want to save the world. Can you say the same?"

I stared at him.

"Deep down, do you actually give a shit about the world, Jolene? Or are you more concerned to trying to tell yourself that you're a good person? We both know the answer to that."

I walked to the door. "Now." I opened it, and he went through wordlessly. I escorted him back down the elevator, to the lobby, and then out the door, ending up in the courtyard again. It was almost ridiculous how much had changed in less than an hour.

I stood there waiting for him to walk away, and he stayed, standing close, looking down at me.

"I'll talk to you soon," he finally said. I breathed a sigh of relief when he started walking away. "Oh," he said, stopping and turning around. "You should learn some wrestling moves."

I shook my head. "Are you flirting with me now? Seriously?"

He laughed. "No. I was thinking about what you said earlier about how your reaction time still sucks. You knock them down, disorient them with that first impact, right?" I nodded. "Okay, but you can't punch 'em once you've got 'em down. Learn a few good wrestling holds, and as strong as you are nobody'd be able to get away from you."

I thought about it. "That might just work."

"Course it will."

"Okay. Thanks for the tip."

He took a breath. "That was given in good faith, Jolene. I hope you understand that you can trust me. Not many people can; I'll admit that. But I want you to trust me."

"I'll keep that in mind."

Connor shook his head, then turned and finally walked away. I walked quickly back into Command. I looked once more out the front doors to make sure he'd actually gone, then I made my way back up to my suite. It was a lot to process. As I rode back up the elevator, my mind just kept spinning. The guy I was pretty sure I was sort of, maybe, starting to fall in love with was a former super villain. He was also determined to keep this going, apparently whether I was sure I wanted him around or not. I've read a few romances where the things he'd said to me just now would have come across as sexy and romantic, but this wasn't like that. I couldn't explain it. I just knew that I didn't feel flattered, or sexy, or excited about him at the moment.

I guessed it was the combination of "hey, I was a really bad super villain!" and "this isn't over" that had me feeling that way. I just knew I needed to put the brakes on. I needed to stop daydreaming about him all the time. Maybe it would all work out. Maybe he'd somehow convince me that he was who I thought he was, and we'd move forward.

But I was starting to think that he never was who I'd thought he was.

I shook my head. "Making all Mama's mistakes, even though you know better. Pretty smart, Jolene," I muttered to myself.

# CHAPTER THREE

After my chat with Connor, all I wanted to do was hide in my bed. Preferably forever. Or, better yet, wake up and find that all of it had been one of my stupid nightmares. I'd fallen into bed for a few hours of fitful sleep, then dragged myself out of bed so Caine and I could do our patrol shift. I wasn't in the mood to talk, and Caine seemed to catch on to that pretty quickly. We did most of our shift in silence, and when we got back to Command, I headed to the elevator without a word.

"Jo," Caine called after me, and I turned around.

"Yeah?"

He caught up to me. "You okay?"

I shook my head. "Tired. I'm sorry if I was a bitch today."

He shrugged. "No more than usual."

I gave him a sidelong glance. "That could be taken a couple of ways."

"It could."

I glanced at him again, and he gave me a small smile, just the barest lift of the corner of his mouth. "You're not a bitch," he finally said.

"I probably am sometimes."

He shrugged. "I think if you were nice and upbeat all the time you'd get on every damn one of my nerves during our patrol shifts. Do you know who my old patrol partner was?"

I shook my head.

"Portia. And she's very no nonsense now, but she's also one of those people who thinks mornings are just great and likes to talk the entire way through a shift."

"So... she's pleasant?" I asked. We got to the elevator and I pushed the button to take us down to the bottom floor. I was starving.

"Yeah."

"How awful," I said as we stepped onto the elevator.

"You have no idea. Because then I'd have to be nice too, and we both know I'm not exactly Mr. Congeniality."

"Is there a point to this?" I asked, and he gave a low laugh.

"I'm just saying, you're not a bitch. You're you. That's all."

I studied him. He kept his dark eyes on the numbers above the doors.

"Well, you're not a bitch, either," I finally said.

"Thanks. I was worried," he said wryly.

"I know it was keeping you up at night."

He shook his head and got off on his floor, and I went downstairs and grabbed a quick bite to eat in the cafeteria. I was thinking I might catch a nap after my crappy night's sleep the night before, while everything was quiet

I was about to hit the button for the elevator to go back up to my floor when I glanced toward the weight room. It was usually pretty empty — these weren't exactly gym rat superheroes on our team. Beta was in there, and I'd run into him while working out before. I shrugged and walked into the weight room. I could nap later.

Probably.

"Hey, Daystar," he said, blowing out a puff of breath as he pushed the barbell above him again, doing a bench press.

"You know you're supposed to have someone spotting you," I said.

"Never had anyone around here other than Caine who set foot in here before. Besides, I don't think there's much risk of getting hurt," he said, lowering the barbell.

"Still. It hurts like a bitch if it falls on you," I said. I went and stood near his head, ready to take the barbell if he had any trouble with it. He was lifting a lot. Not as much as I could, but a decent amount for a non-super strength type. His face was flushed, and he was sweating, his short hair sticking up at crazy angles.

"You ever had that happen?" he asked.

"Yep. In the first gym I used to go to, where I started lifting. Scared the hell out of me, too. I was sure I was going to die there. I had this bruise across my chest for weeks afterward."

"You probably cracked something," he grunted.

"Probably," I agreed.

"You didn't go to the doctor?"

"Yeah, right. Tell my mother I hurt myself lifting weights at the gym where they trained boxers? She would have had a conniption fit."

He chuffed out a short laugh, and I held my hand out as he settled the bar on the stand. He sat up, grabbed a towel, and wiped some of the sweat from his face. "Daystar, I — "

"Why do you still call me that? You know what my actual name is," I pointed out.

He gave me a small smile. "Because we all call each other by our code names. It's a habit and now it's weird actually knowing someone's name." He stuck his hand out toward me. "David Fendrath," he said.

I shook my head. "Jolene Faraday. Which you already knew," I reminded him. We shook hands, and I motioned for him to get up so I could do a set. I added some weight to the bar, and he grimaced.

"Seriously?"

"Uh huh."

"It's a good thing I'm totally confident of my manhood," he muttered as he watched me add more. "Mostly," he added.

I laughed and settled myself onto the bench. He stood near my head, where I'd been standing for him. This reminded me of the camaraderie I'd found at my old gym. Most of the guys there either teased me, flirted with me, or aggressively suggested that I find a "lady gym" to work out at. But the few who were decent to me had been a lot like Beta.... David. It was going to be hard to remember to call him that. We'd talk, or not talk, and it was all fine.

"It hurts just looking at that," he said as I lifted a second time. I glanced at his face to see him watching the bar, tense, ready to grab it.

"You know, if I drop it, I'll be fine," I said.

"Still. It'll hurt. Uh. Right? I mean, you feel pain."

"I do," I said, straightened my arms to lift it again. I did a couple more, then settled it on the stand and sat up.

"So, Jenson and I have been working on going through those files she found. She's still sure Alpha was up to something. We've found a few files that had extra levels of encryption on them, and I was able to crack a couple of them after a while."

"Anything important?"

He shook his head. "Mostly scouting reports on people he wanted on the team. Including you."

I nodded.

"We're going to keep looking. I don't know what she thinks she saw or heard, but Jenson's positive there's more out there and that he was up to something bad."

"He's your cousin, right?"

He nodded.

"So you know him. Do you think he was up to more?"

He sat beside me and shrugged. "We were never close, you know? I mean, you've dealt with him. He's an asshole of the highest order. He always has been."

"Yet he brought you on here," I pointed out.

"He always got a kick out of bossing the rest of the family around. And his dad was the rich one in our family and he never let anyone forget it. Everything had to be at their house, on their schedule."

"And you all went along with that?"

He let out a short laugh. "Our grandma was a formidable woman. Any sign of infighting, any sign of schism between any of us, and we'd hear about it. For the most part, it wasn't a big deal. Some people just like making everyone around them feel less, somehow, and he and his dad were both like that."

"What about his mom?"

He shrugged. "They didn't talk about her. I was always under the impression that she took off on them shortly after he was born."

I didn't say anything for a while. "But there's more. You actively fought against him with us. That's not just normal family bullshit."

He grabbed a pair of dumb bells and started doing curls. He was silent for a bit, and I was starting to think he wouldn't answer. Maybe he didn't even know why he'd done it.

"When we were ten, a stray cat got hit by a car in front of us. We were in his front yard playing. We saw it happen. I had nightmares about it for weeks afterward. I'm a cat person," he added, and I smiled. "Anyway. We saw it happen, and he laughed. Just cracked up, like it was the funniest thing he'd ever seen. And when he saw how upset I was, he went into the street, picked up the body, and started making it dance. Laughing the whole time," he said. He met my eyes. "I'd like to say that he changed. That he grew out of that kind of lack of empathy. I thought he had. We weren't in contact for several years, not until we both ended up with powers. And I thought he was different. He started this. I thought it was for all the right reasons. He was putting his money to use for something good."

I could see the self-disgust on his face, that he'd been involved. That he hadn't done anything to change the way things were done. That he hadn't seen what was happening right under this nose. "I didn't know that he had Caine and Toxxin collared that whole time." Caine, Toxxin, and a few other prisoners under Alphas's reign had been dampened, wearing thin metal "collars" that interfered with the ability to access their powers. He'd done the same thing to me. The difference was that I had always been dampened, whereas Caine and Toxxin's collars had been a threat, a way to easily control them if they looked like they were about to do anything other than what Alpha wanted.

"I didn't know he was doing that shit until you," he said quietly, meeting my eyes. "And then when I started cracking some of those files..." he shook his head. "I'm sorry, Jolene."

"I'm glad you didn't know," I said. "You were nice to me my first day here. I would have been really pissed off if the whole asshole thing had been something that ran in the family."

He laughed a little. "I feel like an idiot."

"Well. I don't think anyone knew what to do. Even those who did know what he was doing, you know? I mean, Jenson sort of knew and she didn't do anything about it. Portia knew. I don't think there's a protocol for what a superhero team should do when they realize their leader is the type of thing they're supposed to be fighting."

"Yeah. But you stepped up," he said, watching me.

"Well. I'm not a superhero," I said with a smile, and he shook his head. "Keep me updated on anything you find, okay?"

"I will." He paused, then kind of ducked his head, like he was embarrassed or something.

"What?" I asked.

"Nothing."

I kept watching him, and he finally shook his head and laughed. "Fine. I was wondering if I've done something to piss Jenson off."

"Jenson?"

"I can't get her to talk to me lately, like, at all. And I've tried."

I studied him. "Jenson isn't the most talkative person in the world. Unless she's telling my ass off about something."

"Yeah, I know. But we've gotten pretty close in the past few years and we're usually great. But lately she seems to actively avoid me."

"And are you actively not avoiding her?" I asked with a grin."So cute."

"I'm trying."

I laughed.

"She doesn't realize it, does she?" he asked.

"No. I'm pretty sure she doesn't," I said.

"Good."

"Why?"

"She's a good friend. We work really well together. We pretty much know what the other one is gong to say before it's said. I don't want to lose that, and she's not looking for a relationship. She steers clear of that kind of thing."

I nodded, remembering Jenson telling me pretty much the same thing. I patted his hand. "Well, it's too bad, really. I think you two would be ridiculously dorky and adorable together."

"Thanks. I think." He stood up and went to the door, and I followed him. "We'll get this all worked out. It'll be fine," he told me.

I nodded. "About Jenson… get her involved in helping you with those files. She loves that kind of stuff, and maybe if you're working on something together, she'll open up a little. Or not. She's not the most open person."

He nodded. "Thanks for the tip. And for not saying anything."

"Sure."

I got up and started to leave. "If you're able to crack any more of those files, let me know."

"Not if. When," he said.

"Oh, sorry," I said, grinning at him.

"You should get some sleep. You look exhausted," he said, and I nodded. We walked out of the training room and I headed up to my suite. I did get into bed, but then I ended up thinking, unable to turn my mind off, thinking about all of the crap Connor had told me the night before. I got back up, kicking off my covers, and grabbed my laptop from the living room.

I crawled back into bed and did a search for "Raider."

A lot of what I found was the current Raider, of course. She was vicious, vindictive, and, from the articles I read and what I'd already heard about her, she got a kick out of causing pain. Of scaring her prey, of messing with them the way a cat toys with a mouse.

I tried not to spend too much time wondering how it was that Connor had been married to someone like that. People change.

Right.

After a while, I found older articles about the original Raider. Newspaper articles, blog posts. Official dispatches from law enforcement. The first newspaper article had a full color photograph of Raider... Connor. The uniform was similar to the one the current Raider wore, midnight black with slashes of blood red across the arms and torso, a black mask that left the mouth and chin exposed. Two long, deadly-looking swords were sheathed at his hips, blades glinting in the glow of a nearby street lamp. In the photograph, Connor as Raider stood over a body, the line of his mouth grim, angry, fists clenched like he was hoping the guy would get up so he could hurt him again. I looked for the caption.

*The super villain known as Raider moments after killing London's Marvel, who was the leader of the city's superhero team, Legion.*

44

I felt sick to my stomach. I clasped my shaking hands in my lap and stared at the caption. "Damn it, Connor," I whispered. I sorted through more articles. Lots of articles about how hated Raider and his team were, about how they'd singlehandedly destroyed entire neighborhoods in parts of England, Ireland, and Scotland. After a while, I set my laptop down on the bed, rested my elbows on my knees, and stared at the screen without seeing it.

How did I reconcile this? How did I put this sadistic super villain together with the man who watched over my mother when I couldn't, who sent me ugly socks and pestered Jenson, politely, until she let him see me when I was in the hospital? Someone who could cause that kind of damage with the man who kissed me in a way that made me feel like I was flying without ever leaving the ground?

I stared at the photo of him as Raider. To believe it was possible, I had to believe that people could change. I didn't know if I had it in me to believe that. I've certainly never seen anyone change that much, especially not over the course of just a few years. And his demeanor the previous night hadn't exactly made me feel much better about it.

This. This right here is why I've been single for so long.

I sat there for a while longer, until I heard someone knocking on my door. I got up and looked out to see Jenson in the corridor, and I opened up.

"You look exhausted," Jenson said in greeting.

"I am. Lot of crap on my mind."

She sat down and I sat on the couch next to her. She was still in her full uniform, which meant she'd probably just gotten back from a patrol shift. "How'd it go?" I asked her.

"We had a Daemon sighting." Daemon was one of Dr. Death's teammates. Another of the several villains who just kept slipping away from us. "Amy actually did a good job trying to capture him, but he got whisked away by their teleporter again."

"I hate that," I muttered, and she nodded.

"What's bugging you? Why so tired?" she asked.

I shrugged. "Bad dreams. Stuff on my mind." Killjoy, mainly, but I didn't feel like talking about that, like telling Jenson, who had her shit together more than anyone I'd ever known, that I'd gotten myself involved with a former super villain and I was still trying to figure out how okay I was with that. Then I remembered Connor's advice. "Do we have anyone who can teach me some wrestling holds?"

"Yeah. Your partner. He has training in all of that stuff."

I wanted to laugh. Of course. Considering he already had a bug up his ass about how much time I was spending with Caine, Connor would just love hearing that I'd be spending even more time with him now.

"Thanks. I'll ask him."

I just ran into Beta," Jenson said. "He asked me to tell you that he went back to his lab after you two talked earlier and he thinks he made some progress on a couple of Alpha's files."

"Seriously? We should go check it out."

"What? Now?"

"Now. The sooner we get some questions answered, the sooner we can get Alpha, Nightbane, and Crystal moved to international confinement."

We headed down to the second floor, which was where David's lab was. When he wasn't officially on duty, he could almost always be found there, and he'd been responsible for working on some of our newer tech, as well as security stuff. Jenson and I walked into the lab and found David in his usual place, head bent over his keyboard as he tapped away. He looked up when he heard the door whoosh open.

"Hey, Jolene," he said, sitting up. He transferred his gaze to Jenson. "Hey Jenson," he added, his tone changing a little. I was pretty sure he was blushing and it was kind of ridiculously cute.

"Hey. How's it going?" I asked as I hid a smile, and Jenson gave him a small nod.

"Okay. I think I'm making some headway on those encrypted files."

"Yeah?"

"Yeah. Look at this," he said, waving us over. Jenson and I went next to where he was sitting and I bent down so I could see the monitor he was pointing out. "This was the first file I was able to crack."

I started reading. "It's an email or something."

"Yeah. Keep reading."

I glanced at him. The tension in his voice sent a trickle of fear down my spine. I looked back at the monitor. A lot of it was bullshit about weather and vacation spots and stuff, and then, toward the end of the document, there was a short paragraph: "Regarding your inquiry about the possibility of sharing samples and information, I must admit that I'm intrigued. Especially at the price you offered. As you know, I have many exceptional samples at my disposal, collected for much the reasons you stated. At this time, I will have to decline, as I believe my assets are worth a bit more than even your generous offer. I'm sure you understand. However, I would be willing to consider it for an increased offer. We can continue these discussions when I return from Paris. Cordially, Michael A. Fendrath."

"Michael is Alpha?" I asked.

"Yeah."

"Samples. So someone was offering him what I guess was a lot of money for samples of something. Any idea what?"

He clicked, opening another document. "This was the next one. Looks like an inventory. See what you think, and I'm going to hope it's different from what I think."

I bent down again, and he stood and offered me his chair. "Thanks," I murmured as I looked at the screen and Jenson crouched next to me to read. David stood just behind me as I started reading.

It was a spreadsheet. In one column, there was a list of things:

Self-Replication
Invisibility
Super Strength
Super Speed
Contact Toxicity
Heightened Senses
Flight
Alter Outcomes
Teleportation

In the next column, a list of amounts, corresponding to the items in the first column. Numbers in the millions. And in the final column, it looked like some kind of ranking, from one to five.

"Powers of the original StrikeForce members," I murmured, matching up the power with the hero. "My guess is the second column is a dollar amount. And if I'd known y'all were worth this much, I'd have sold you myself," I said, and Jenson shook her head. "I think the final column is some kind of ranking, but it doesn't say of what." I turned and looked at David. "Is that what you were thinking?"

He nodded, then looked up at the ceiling.

"Did he... so he was talking about samples in the first file. Did he mean, like you guys in particular? Or do you think he meant like blood or DNA samples? Did he even have anything like that?"

And then I remembered. He did. He had DNA. Because one of the very first things I'd had to do was submit to a mouth swab when they'd forced me to join.

"He took blood from us, too," Jenson said. "In the med wing. He had us give blood, he said, to bank it for if we ever lost too much and needed a transfusion."

"They never took mine," I said.

David nodded. "I was able to dig into the metadata. This list was written before you were on the team. These are all individual powers. You have a bunch of them. And I think the dollar figure beside your powers would have been significantly higher, based on what they were talking about for these," he said, nodding toward the screen.

I closed my eyes. "I think it's probably too much to hope that his contact was someone working for the good guys."

"Yeah."

"Any idea who it was yet?" I asked, opening my eyes to look at him.

"Not yet. But I'm not resting until I crack the rest of this mess."

Jenson and I stayed and chatted with David for a couple of minutes, and then we started back up toward my suite. We were just getting off the elevator when Portia came on my comm.

"Daystar?"

"Yep. What's up, Portia?" I asked.

"We have a Dr. Death sighting near Midtown. Do you want it?"

"Hell yeah," I said, quickening my pace. Jenson did the same.

"Figured so. We'll meet you in the meeting room."

"Copy," I said. I dashed back to my room to change into my uniform, and then we made our way through the corridors, up the stairwell to the floor where the team meting room was. When we got to the room with its sleek black table, walls of glass, and arrays of monitors, Portia, Amy, Monica, Dani, and Toxxin were already there.

"What, we're all going?"

"If it's him, we're gonna make sure we get the bastard," Monica said from where she was perched on the table beside Dani. "Caine and Beta are staying here."

"I want another crack at him, without a doubt," Toxxin said, and I nodded.

"Let's go then," Portia said. The next second, we were standing behind one of the parking lots near the Detroit Institute of Arts. The museum was lit up, white limestone glowing in the night. Across the street was the main branch of the Detroit Public Library, more limestone.

"We've got a report of an alarm in the art museum," Beta said over our comms. When Jenson wasn't on, watching and directing from Command, it was usually Beta. David. I would eventually get used to using my teammates' actual names. "I'm looking at the security feed now. We got Dr. Death and Daemon near the Kresge Court."

"Try not to break any art," Jenson muttered to me as we moved, running, keeping to the shadows toward the nearest entrance.

"I've alerted the security guards that you're on your way," Beta said.

"Thank you," Portia told him. I glanced around at our group. Portia was the tallest of us, wearing a half mask, a gray arrow insignia on her chest. Amy, who'd decided to go with the code name "Steel," had already turned to metal, which I thought was the single most awesome power any of us had, because she looked freaking deadly. Monica, AKA "Swoon," had a wavy line as her insignia, representing her telekinetic powers. Dani's red hair flowed from beneath her cowl, and she had a shard of broken glass as her insignia. Screamer. They were silent, serious, and I was surprised to find that I was glad they were with me.

"Okay. Let's do this."

"Try not to break anything," David said over our comms.

"We know, man," Monica said.

"I was mostly talking to Jolene," he said.

"Seriously. Why do you all assume I'm just gonna break shit?"

Jenson cleared her throat, smothering a laugh, and I rolled my eyes. Portia tried the door.

"Still locked."

I stepped forward and gave the handle a hard pull, and the door swung open. "Not anymore," I said, and we walked in. We were in a lobby area, and there was a short staircase straight ahead.

"Knights and armor is in that gallery," Jenson said quietly. "Rivera Court is just past that." We nodded, and Portia and I exchanged a glance.

"I'll do my thing," I said.

"You do that," Portia said with a slight smile. I rose into the air and flew through the museum, past the large, open gallery that held glass cases full of medieval armor and weapons, though to be honest, if the situation had been different, I would have stayed in there longer. Seeing the elaborate coffered ceiling up close was the kind of thing I was grateful to my powers for. I could see things other people never got to see, not the way I could.

Another day, maybe. I swooped toward the Rivera Court.

"Jolene, security updated us. They're in the Egyptian gallery upstairs now. Third floor. Death is messing with one of the sarcophagi in there."

"Ew. Meet me there," I said.

"Copy."

It was easy to find my way up once I figured out where the staircases were. I took it up, flying just above the floor, since I could fly so much faster than I could walk or run.

"Are they still there?" I asked, pressing my comm.

"Yeah. We're on two now."

"Move your asses unless you want me to have all the fun," I said. I picked up speed. I could see the Egyptian gallery straight ahead of me now, statues of scribes, pharaohs, and, in the smaller gallery beyond, mummy cases. I could hear something scraping, low voices.

"Hold that," I heard a male voice say, and then I burst into the gallery, through the wide doorway. Daemon and Dr. Death were there, Daemon holding some kind of stone sculpture in his hands, looking bored, which, on my limited contact with him, was how he usually looked. Death was rummaging through the nearby display case, and he picked something up. They both seemed to notice that I was there at the same time, and I made my move. Of the two, as far as I knew, Daemon was the more powerful, so I plowed into him, knocking him into the side of a large stone sarcophagus that sat in the center of the room. His head hit it with a hard thunk and he went limp. I tossed him to the floor and took a step toward Dr. Death, who clutched one of those jars that the Egyptians kept body parts in when they mummified people. I couldn't remember the word for it, I just knew it was gross as fuck and the dude had issues if he went through all this trouble to get some kidneys or whatever the hell was in there.

"Stop right there," Dr. Death said, and I smiled. I took another step toward him. I tried to look like I was focusing completely on him. And I was, but I was also trying to keep a look out for his little blond transporter. She always seemed to get them out of trouble at the last moment.

"We're here," Jenson said in my ear. "Just outside."

"Well, at least I didn't find you doing something really inappropriate with the bodies," I said to Dr. Death, and he sneered at me. If he wasn't a psychotic super villain, I guess he could have been considered handsome. He wore a dark suit, black shirt and tie. A fedora pulled low over his dark eyes. Olive complexion, wavy hair peeking from beneath the brim of his hat. Not extremely tall, but muscular looking. He was probably in his late forties, and had that distinguished gentleman look going for him.

Except for the mummified body parts he was holding, of course.

"What are you going to do with that?" I asked him, taking another step.

"This!" he shouted, and threw the jar at me. I dodged it, and the distraction gave him just enough time to bolt for the next gallery.

"Secure that bastard," I said, gesturing toward Daemon as I ran after Dr. Death. I could hear Toxxin behind me, along with Dani.

"Brianne, now," I heard Dr. Death say calmly.

"Fuck," I muttered, and rose into the air so I could move faster. I threw myself at him, grabbing a hold of his arm just as the blond appeared and whisked him away.

The only thing was, because I was holding onto him, this time I went with them. Which would end up being either a really great move on my part or one of those many things that I'd wish I'd thought through more carefully.

# CHAPTER FOUR

When we reappeared again, I was still clutching Dr. Death, and we were somewhere along the water. Large houses, mansions, loomed across a road, and we stood on the beach near the water.

"Rude, to invite oneself along where they aren't wanted," Dr. Death murmured, his calm, cultured tone making me want to punch him in the face even more than usual. More quickly than I would have imagined, he wrenched himself out of my grip, but I had just enough time to hit him in the face before he darted away. He bent over, blood dripping from his nose and onto the wet sand near his feet.

"Get that bitch," he told his teleporter. Brianne.

"Where are you?" Jenson asked in a panicky voice in my comm.

"Jo?" Caine's voice rumbled over the comm a moment later. Even if I'd wanted to answer him, I didn't have a chance to as I saw the glint of a gun in the blond's hand. I lunged, knocking into her. I heard the gun go off, but if she had managed to shoot at me, my uniform had protected me.

"Not nice. Super villains never have any goddamn manners," I said as she struggled against me, trying to wrench herself out of my grasp. I held on tighter. She was bigger, bulkier than I am, and she knew how to fight, how to try to maneuver herself out of a situation.

But she wasn't as strong as me. It crossed my mind that Connor had been right, that even untrained, my strength worked if I let it work for me this way. It wasn't as fun as punching, but it would maybe get the job done.

I felt an impact on my back and realized Dr. Death was kicking me as I wrestled with his teammate. I snarled as he landed another one, right in my ribs. I swore I felt something crack, and I let out a shout.

"Let go," he ordered, kicking me again. I winced, but held on, wrestled her as I kicked out at him,

"Jo, we have your location. They're on their way," Caine said in my ear. "Hold on."

The blond stopped struggling in my arms, going limp. I didn't trust her enough to let go. It could have been an act, and there wasn't a chance in hell I was letting her get away. She was the reason, every single time we came up against Mayhem, that they were able to get away from us. Not because we were overpowered or fought badly, necessarily, but because they had this easy getaway, via the blond. Not anymore. The broken ribs would be worth it to make sure she didn't help Mayhem out anymore.

I kicked out at Dr. Death again, catching his shin. It was pure luck. I was flailing, just hoping I managed to land a kick. He howled and stepped back.

"You're going to pay for this," he shouted at me, blood from his nose dripping down his face. I kept a hand tangled in the blond's hair and lunged toward him when it became clear that he wanted to run. He danced out of my reach, and ran off into the night.

Just then, Portia and the others appeared, and I breathlessly gestured in the direction he'd gone, and everyone except Steel and Jenson took off in pursuit.

"Take her. We have a dampener?" I asked. Steel nodded and fastened it around the transporter's neck. I stood up, holding my ribs. I grimaced, then rose into the air in the direction Dr. Death had taken.

We searched the beach, the water, any docks or boathouses nearby for nearly an hour, but we eventually had to admit that we'd lost any sign of him.

"You did good, girl," Monica said as we walked back. I held my ribs again.

"Not good enough. The fucker got away."

"We're too slow," Dani said angrily. "We should have been there helping you instead of you having to deal with them yourself."

"We're still new at this shit," I said. "It's not a big deal. I should have tried to grab his foot when he was kicking me. And we got two of them," I said, looking at the scene on the beach, where Portia and Amy were standing over the transporter and Daemon. Both of them wore dampening collars and Daemon was conscious, but seemed out of it, shaking his head.

"He got away," I told Portia.

"We got these two though," Portia said, putting her fist out, and I bumped mine to it.

"*Daystar* got these two," Dani said, and I shook my head.

"If you guys hadn't been there, I wouldn't have gotten to them in time at all," I said. "I just wish we'd gotten Dr. Death. I can't believe he took off so fast."

"We got his free ride, though," Jenson said, nodding toward the blond. "That's only going to make our lives easier."

"Yep," I said. "Any idea who she is?"

"Running her face through the recognition program now. It takes a while sometimes."

"Well, let's get them back. Steel, I assume you want to be present for their questioning?" Portia asked, and Amy nodded.

"Me, too," I said, and nobody disagreed with me. Portia transported us back to Command, directly to the detention facility. My former guard, Marie, was on duty, and she greeted us, helped us get first Daemon and then the transporter, Brianne, into cells. I watched as Marie fastened them into chairs exactly like the one I had spent far too much time in not all that long ago, wrists and ankles shackled to the chair. Later, they'd be fitted with adult diapers, the whole deal. I supposed I should have felt bad for them, having gone through it all myself, but I couldn't find it in myself to feel anything but satisfaction. Dr. Death and Mayhem had caused the deaths of over thirty people just a few weeks ago when he'd set off some crazy machine in Midtown. At the time, he'd taunted StrikeForce, telling them that the machine would make ordinary people into super powered people, super powered people under his command. Instead, the machine had seemingly fried them from the insides, out. The team had been so desperate, they'd let me out of jail to go after him. He and most of his cronies had gotten away thanks to Brianne, leaving Maddoc behind to deal with me.

And deal with me, he had. But I had the last laugh, and Maddoc was now rotting here in detention.

"We have an ID on the transporter," Jenson said quietly as she approached me. She held her tablet up, and a color photo of the blond was on the screen. A bit younger, with make up on, and her her hair piled luxuriously on top of her head, but her just the same. The name "Brianne Montfort" was on the screen. Born a few years before me in Toronto.

"She's been missing for almost ten years. Her parents and fiancee reported her missing, and the authorities never made any progress. There are some mysterious gaps in the file from the investigation, officers who went missing."

"Probably officers who learned something," I said.

"Exactly. Her parents kept her powers a secret from the police at first, but eventually they realized it would help the investigation. Teleportation, like we figured. Exceptionally quick at it. Portia is great, but we've both seen this one in action. It's scary how little effort it seems to take her," Jenson continued as we watched Brianne getting strapped into her chair as we stood outside the door of her cell. "We have no idea if she's been with Mayhem the whole time. We didn't even know she existed until you saw her that time."

I nodded, keeping my eyes on her.

"And what's Daemon's thing again?"

"A very particular type of mental manipulation. He makes you see, makes you feel like you're living your worst fears," Jenson said.

"Shit."

"Indeed. There's a long list of suicides that have been attributed to Daemon's influence. From what we understand, he amuses himself greatly pushing people to their deaths."

"What are the odds you think Amy will leave us alone in his cell with him?"

"Why?"

"So I can hit him really, really hard a few times without her objecting," I said.

She shook her head, letting out a short laugh. "I don't think your chances are great."

Marie walked out of the room. "Okay, she's all secured. The collar is secure, and we added a second for back up, since she's a high risk prisoner."

"Thanks, Marie," I said.

"Anytime. She's all yours."

Jenson and I walked into the cell. Amy was already there, sitting in a chair near the door. She nodded at us as we walked in. Portia walked in behind us.

"The rest of the team are keeping an eye on the other one," Portia said. Then she turned to Brianne, who was glaring at all of us, but more specifically at me.

"Don't be pissed at me. It's not my fault he insisted on running like a wuss rather than fighting me. If he had any balls at all, you wouldn't have been involved," I told her with a shrug.

"Ms. Montfort, your cooperation here would be helpful, and it will help you as well. It will factor into how long you're held here, and under what conditions," Portia began.

"Screw yourself. I'm not telling you a damn thing," Brianne said, still glaring at me.

"How did you get involved with Mayhem?" Portia asked. Brianne rolled her eyes.

"When did you meet Dr. Death?" she asked, and received nothing but stony silence.

"I wonder what her super villain name was," I said, and she looked at me the way people usually look at maggots or cockroaches. It's not the first time someone's looked at me that way. Still, I'd be lying if I didn't admit that it pissed me off a little. "Lemme guess. I'm so good at shit like this." I studied her, and the rest of my teammates stayed quiet. "You'd go with something girly. Princess? Lady Ghost? Sparkletits?"

I heard a sound behind me that sounded suspiciously like Jenson choking back a laugh. Brianne continued to glare at me.

"Nah, not that," I said. "Maybe something more along the lines of 'Fido.' Just come when he calls you, like a dog?"

She moved like she wanted to hit me, and I hid a smile. "That one struck a nerve, huh? Well, you were loyal, I'll give you that. Dependable. When he called, you came. Impressive, really." There was no disgust now. Now there was just hatred. "Must sting a little, though. Little rich girl, driving a Porsche through your lakeside neighborhood, and then you find yourself here in Detroit, at some creepy guy's beck and call." I stopped talking, let the silence linger. Brianne continued to glare at me.

"Someone treated me that way, I'd want to see them get their comeuppance," Portia said quietly. "This would be a good time to save yourself, Ms. Montfort. We have you. We have Daemon. We have Maddoc. Without you out there helping him, it's just a matter of time until we get Dr. Death and the rest of Mayhem. You help us, and we'll make sure you don't spend any more time here than necessary," Portia said. It was all bullshit of course. There was no pre-determined "necessary" amount of time we kept them in detention. Amy was the representative here on the prisoners' behalves, and as fair as she wanted to be, she recognized that some of those we took in just shouldn't be allowed to be free and able to cause pain and chaos. We'd started the process of working with the international super hero community to get our prisoners transferred to a more neutral, better-equipped prison, but it was kind of a long process and we weren't especially ready to hand Alpha over yet. Not until David and Jenson figured out what he'd been up to. Still, it's not like Brianne knew that, so we all played along.

"I'm not telling you anything," Brianne repeated, and then she closed her eyes and turned her face away from us. Portia and I glanced at one another. We wouldn't be getting anything out of her, at least not at first. I nodded toward the door, and we all filed out.

"We'll try again tomorrow," Portia said after the door whooshed closed behind us.

"I'm not expecting much from Daemon," I said as we walked toward his cell.

"I hate this guy," Jenson said as we stood outside his cell door. "He's creepy and he looks at you like he can see you naked."

"Well, he can't. Not now. He can say shit, but he can't make us see and feel things the way he usually would," Portia said. She hit a button, and his cell door opened.

Like Brianne, Daemon was strapped to the large metal chair in the center of the cylindrical shaped cell. Unlike Brianne, though, he looked at us calmly, a slight smile on his face as he watched us file into his cell. It was impossible to tell his age. He had a sharp, stark looking face, a tall, lanky build, and short dark hair. Narrow dark eyes. He was unnaturally calm for someone in his situation, and my skin crawled just being in the cell with him.

"Ah, the infamous Daystar," he said, ignoring everyone else. "Your fears were fun. You were terrified of losing your mother, of disappointing her. Of being helpless." He smiled. "How is your Mama doing?"

I lunged toward him, and Amy held me back, her body going to steel, meeting the impact of my strength with strength of her own.

"He's strapped down, Daystar," she said calmly. "Cool it, or I'm going to ask you to leave."

I stopped struggling, stopped trying to get to the bastard. I stepped back. "Sorry," I muttered to Amy, and she patted my shoulder. She turned to Daemon.

"I'll tell you this now, mister. I'm here, and I'm here to try to make sure you get a fair shake. But if you piss that one off, there's not much any of us can do to stop her from getting to you. So I'd watch it."

"She's too weak. She'd never actually do anything to anyone who couldn't defend himself. Trying to be honorable, when really, there isn't a noble bone in her body."

"You're right. There's not," I said, crossing my arms to keep from trying to throttle him. "You'd be surprised what I'm perfectly okay with doing," I added, and he kept that same self-satisfied smirk on his face, his eyes on mine. Creepy little shit.

"We're here for information. We have you, your transporter, and Maddoc. Mayhem is just about at an end. If you help us clean up some loose ends, we'll remember that when it comes to your sentencing," Portia said. "And when it comes to the treatment you receive here. The freedoms you'll be granted."

He just kept looking at me. "You should be afraid, Daystar," he said in that creepy calm voice. "So much to lose, am I right?"

I clenched my fists. All of my focus was on keeping my expression blank, on not dropping my gaze, not allowing him even that small victory.

"So afraid," he repeated. "All of you are. That Caine asshole. I saw his fears that day, and he's pathetic. Toxxin, afraid of being alone for the rest of her life because she can't touch anybody," he said with a laugh. "It was fun messing with her mind, making her see herself as an old woman, dying alone in squalor. Beta's terrified of being alone with Alpha, you know that?" He paused, and then he grinned. "Of course, I know all of Dr. Death's fears, too. Virus's as well."

I kept my face blank again. Virus. Damian. My former burgling partner. He'd joined up with Mayhem after they'd approached him about forming a business relationship, one where he could make a lot more money than he made with me, since I refused to just take everything we could. We hadn't been the best match in terms of business strategy, I guess. As far as I knew, none of them knew that the woman they'd seen once at Damian's mansion, his former partner, was also the superhero known as Daystar. Of course, who knew what the hell Damian had told them?

"I know their fears," Daemon repeated quietly, still with that creepy little smile on his face. "It's knowledge I'm willing to share. For a price."

"What's your price?" Portia asked.

He grinned wider. "My freedom. What else would I want?"

Portia shook her head. "That's just stupid. You know we're not going to do that."

"Then you're not really all that serious about ending Mayhem and bringing Dr. Death in now, are you? The lives of all those people he killed, they just don't balance against my life. I should feel special, but mostly I'm disgusted by how pathetic you 'superheroes' are."

"My god do you ever stop talking?" I asked, and then regretted it when he looked at me again.

"Why would I do that, when I'm so good at it? Look how I have all of you squirming, even though you've dampened my powers. So weak, so afraid. I don't even need to manipulate you worthless bitches. You're your own worst enemies, aren't you?"

I wanted to hit him. Hard. The thing that pissed me off the most, probably, was that he was right. I hated it when others pointed out my weaknesses. I knew them all too well without anyone spelling them out for me.

"Telepaths are pretty much the worst," Jenson said.

"If you say so. Why don't you tell me something, Jenson? That's what you go by? I couldn't detect a single thing you were afraid of. Why is that?"

I glanced at Jenson, who, I had to admit, looked a lot calmer than anyone else in the room. She just shrugged. "Maybe you're not as good as you thought you were."

We questioned him for a few more minutes, then gave up when all he gave us was a bunch of bullshit none of us especially wanted to hear. We filed out of his cell, and Portia stopped in the corridor outside. "We'll keep working on both of them. In the meantime, we work harder to track Dr. Death down. He's going to stick to the shadows now, which is never a good thing because every time he's finally left the shadows, something bad has happened. We need to find him, like, yesterday."

"I need to meet with David, so I'll fill him in," Jenson said, then, without another word, she stepped into the elevator and left.

"Get some rest. Go to the med wing and have your ribs looked at, Daystar," Portia said as she headed toward the other elevator.

"I'm fine," I said.

"Uh huh," she said as she walked into the elevator. She turned and crossed her arms. "Go to the med wing," she told me. The doors closed, and I rolled my eyes.

"So are you going or are we going to have to drag you kicking and screaming to get them looked at?" Amy asked.

"Ugh. You too?"

"I'm just watching my own ass here. If you're too messed up, I might actually have to fight something. Who needs it?" she asked with a grin.

"Fine. I'm going."

One trip to the med wing showed that I had a couple of hairline fractures and to stay in bed at least over night. After the observations they'd made when I was hospitalized after my fight with Maddoc, they'd realized that I had some accelerated healing. Not like what Connor had, where cuts would heal as I watched, as if he'd never been injured at all. But I healed faster than a non-powered person; most of us seemed to, actually. Once I was finished with that, I stumbled up to my suite, showered and fell into bed. After calling to check in on Mama, I drifted off into a fitful sleep full of nightmares about super villains and my mother and Connor and blood on my hands.

# CHAPTER FIVE

I was patrolling, my second shift of the day. I'd finished my early morning run with Caine, and then Dani had begged me to fill in for her during her shift with Portia, and, like a complete pushover, I agreed. Really, it wasn't so bad, especially times like this, when I was flying over Midtown, looking down at the Wayne State campus and the main branch of the library. Portia was in the minijet, covering her part of our patrol zone while keeping in pretty steady contact with me. StrikeForce had this part of our job, at least, pretty much down to a science. We'd meet first thing in the morning, and Portia would split up the city, giving us each an area to patrol. I flew over mine, but the rest of the team managed with the small, agile helicopters and hoverjets that Alpha had purchased when he'd first started the team. David, Jenson, and Caine, as well as Portia, all knew how to fly them, so they'd fly them when we needed it. I was grateful every shift for my flying ability; I hated being in the jet with Caine, and I usually only rode with him when we had a prisoner we needed to transport.

Of course, I usually ended up going out on calls even when it wasn't my shift, like today. Me, or Caine, since we both had the highest strength on the team. David was out a lot, too. Even though he wasn't quite as strong as us, he was close, and he made up for any lack of strength with his smarts and tech.

I flew over the Detroit Medical Center, where Mama worked, and remembered that I needed to call her later, then I maneuvered back toward Wayne State. I circled over it a few times, barely noting the phones held up to film me, the calls of "Daystar! Down here!" People loved taking selfies with Portia and the others, and I guess Alpha had been big on having his photo taken, but that's just not something I do. I would feel like an asshole.

I was about to circle back and start checking around the art museum and library when I saw dark smoke rising from one of the few remaining houses near the university. Just off of the freeway, there was a block of rickety-looking old houses, usually split up into quads. One of them, a large house with chipping white paint on its clapboard sidings, was spouting smoke from its second-story windows. There was a fire truck on the scene, an ambulance, and two Detroit Police squad cars. I came in for a landing. House fires and other emergencies weren't technically our problem, but pretty much all of us stopped to see if we could help or not. I guess it's not like that in other cities. Most have pretty strict rules about what super teams can get involved in, and usually it has nothing at all to do with "normal" people. Super people, for the most part, only deal with other super people. But not here. I wonder if that will change eventually, but I kind of hope not.

I mean, what's the point of having a team of people who can handle all kinds of crazy shit if they aren't there to help with the less-crazy stuff as well?

I looked toward the house. A woman was on the front lawn, being held back by two officers. I walked toward them, and one of the officers, a woman who reminded me immediately of Angela Bassett, looked relieved.

"We were just about to put in a call to StrikeForce," she said.

"What's going on?" I asked.

"My baby!" the woman they were holding back screamed, trying again to get free and get at the house.

"There's an eleven year old girl in there. Won't come out. One of yours," the older male officer said.

"One of mine?"

"One of you super people. The fire doesn't seem to be bothering her," the female officer explained, still holding the other woman back.

"Who started the fire?"

"The girl," she answered, and I nodded.

I locked my eyes with the woman who was struggling with the officers, who was watching me with desperation in her eyes. "I'll go get her. Okay?"

She nodded, eyes wide, still terrified.

"Where was she in the house? What floor?" I asked her.

"Second floor. Her room's the one in front. She was in the hallway outside her room last I saw. I thought she was running out right behind me," she said, and then she slumped, weeping. I exchanged a glance with the female officer, then walked toward the house. The front door was hanging open. I pressed a button at the side of my mask, one of the many that made my mask much more than just a disguise. There was night vision for my eyes, noise-reduction settings for situations like when we'd first come across Dani and her screaming powers. The other setting was an air filter, for situations just like this one: I could keep breathing, even in the worst of air quality.

I walked into the dark, smoky house. I could hear the crackle of flames just above me, and I took a breath, sending a silent prayer that the house wouldn't come tumbling down with me in it. I mean, I'd live, probably, but I had a feeling it would hurt.

I took the steps two at a time.

"Hello? Anyone here? I'm from StrikeForce. I'm here to help you," I called. I turned at the top of the stairs. I couldn't see down the hallway, black smoke thick around me. "It's okay. You're not in trouble."

"Yes I am!" a girl's voice called out, desperate. Afraid.

"I have a feeling you didn't do this on purpose," I said. Christ. Eleven years old. I can't even imagine what it would have been like to get my powers at that age. I'd been in my mid twenties, and it had still totally messed with my head, this idea of having powers. Granted, I'd been more than happy to have them, but it still didn't feel real. And it screwed with your body, your moods. It was hard to explain, other than you just feel off, unless you use your powers. I had a sneaking suspicion this girl had probably been feeling that for a while, and then her powers had loosed themselves, whether she meant to use them or not.

"I didn't," she said.

"I know. You can't stay in here. Your mom's worried about you, and this whole place is going to fall down soon if this fire doesn't get put out. The flames might not bother you, but a house falling on you definitely will."

"They're gonna lock me up," she wept.

"No. They're not going to lock you up. Come on. You gotta help me get out of here."

I was holding my hands out in front of me, stepping forward slowly through the black smoke. I felt a brush of someone against my hand, and tried to reach out and grab her, but then I heard footsteps, running to my left, into one of the front bedrooms.

"Oh, come on," I muttered. "Do you want to die here?"

"Maybe!"

I felt my way across the wall until I came to the doorway I assumed she'd run through. I'd taken two steps into the room when I heard the house start creaking ominously.

The floor shifted beneath my feet, and I rose up into the air, just a bit, to keep from falling through if the floor gave.

"Help me here, okay?"

"Just go!"

She was somewhere to my right. If I could just keep her talking, I could probably figure out where she was and grab her.

"You didn't do this on purpose. Everyone knows that. You're not in trouble," I said.

"Oh, bull shit, lady. My mom is gonna kill me."

"She is not," I said. "And watch your language, kid."

"Just leave!" she shouted.

There. I caught a quick glimpse of her moving through the smoke, past me, trying to make her way out to the hallway. I lunged, tackled her around the waist, and she screeched in surprise.

"Time to go," I muttered. I held tightly to her as she shouted at me and flailed, trying to get loose. I could just make out the light across the room that indicated where the windows were. I flew toward them, turning around at the last minute so I hit the glass panes with my back, shielding the girl from the flying shards of glass the best I could. Once we were out, it took a few seconds for my eyes to adjust to the brightness. I could hear shouts below us, applause. I circled around quickly then came in for a landing, trying to land as gently as possible with the girl in my arms. I saw Portia, Jenson, and Amy standing with the officers and the girl's mother. I held onto the girl's arm as I led her over to them.

The firefighters started spraying down the flames near the front of the house. A small crowd had gathered, and they inched forward, trying to hear what we were saying, trying to get photos of me and the girl.

"If you take her photo, I will break your phone. And then I'll break your face," I snarled at them, and they backed off, quickly lowering their phones. The girl looked up at me in surprise. She looked even younger than I remember looking at eleven; thin, petite, with her hair done in long, thin braids. Her face and clothing were stained with dark soot, and her big brown eyes were wide. Fearful. Any attitude she'd had in the house had faded once we'd reached the outside.

"You don't sound like a superhero," she said.

"Probably not," I agreed. I greeted her mother with a nod, watching as she wrapped the girl in her arms, crying, thanking God that she was safe.

"Mom says she set the fire," the female cop said, nodding toward the girl. "That's you-all's jurisdiction."

"What are we supposed to do with her? We don't deal with kids," I said.

"Well, we sure the hell can't do anything with this," the cop replied. "Our luck, we'd bring her in and she'd try to burn the whole damn station down."

"She didn't mean to set the fire," I argued.

"But she did. She set it, and she stayed in that inferno without a single burn on her. How the hell do you expect us to deal with a mess like that?"

"It's not a mess," I said. "She has powers. It's not exactly unheard-of."

"Right. And you guys are much better equipped to deal with this than we are, kid or not," she said. "And that's what's going in my report. We handed her off to Daystar of StrikeForce. The End."

I was about to say something when Portia held her hand up. "Enough," she said in a quiet but commanding tone. "She's right. I'm not any happier about it than you are, but this is our responsibility," she told me. I looked away and crossed my arms.

"Told you they're gonna lock me up!" the girl said, sounding terrified.

"We are not locking you up," I said. "We just need to bring you in until we can figure something out. Right?" I asked Portia.

"Exactly. And I was talking to your mom, and she thinks that's a good idea. Our priority is keeping you and everyone else safe. Okay?"

The girl didn't answer, standing there sniffling instead.

"What's your name?" I asked her.

"Darla," she said after a moment. "And I'm mad at you. Why'd you come after me?"

"Because if I hadn't, you would have died in there, crushed under what's left of your house. Is that what you wanted?"

She didn't answer.

"Is it?" I asked more forcefully.

"No."

"Okay. I didn't want that either. I got you out because it's what we do. We try to help people."

"My daddy says you're not very good at it."

"Well, your daddy's an a— "

Jenson cleared her throat loudly.

"Your daddy's an astute man," I said, glancing at Jenson, who was shaking her head. "Sometimes, we're not. But today, we got you out and that's what matters. And we are not locking you up, and even if they planned on it, I wouldn't let them. Can you trust me?"

"You promise?" she asked.

"Promise."

"Okay," she said.

"Mrs. Johnson," Portia said to Darla's mother, "we'll take her to Command now. Do you want to travel with us, or meet us there?"

"Travel with you? Meaning?"

"Either have Daystar fly you or teleport with us," Portia explained.

Mrs. Johnson looked a little bit green at the prospect. "I'll just drive over, thanks," she said. "I want to bring her father with me anyway. We'll be there soon."

Portia nodded, then thanked the officers and firemen on the scene. The two police officers each shook my hand, and the firefighting crew asked if I'd take a picture with them. I was about to argue when Jenson said "sure she will. Here. I'll take it." There was a crowd of bystanders around now, a good couple dozen or so. They'd pulled up in cars and on bikes. I was starting to get used to that, to the crowds and phones and stupid questions, social media feeds filled with pictures of us, bloggers and live streamers following every possible aspect of our lives. I stood and waited for Jenson to take the stupid picture.

The firefighters thanked her and gathered around me as Jenson stepped back and pointed the firefighter's phone at us. "Smile!" she said, and they did, leaning in, giving the camera the thumbs-up. I stood stock still, glaring at Jenson through my mask. She couldn't see it, of course, but by now she knew me well enough to know that I was giving her a death stare.

"There you go," Jenson said, finishing up and handing the phone back to the firefighter.

"Marry me, Daystar," one of the firefighters called, and the others whistled.

"You must have a deathwish, man," I muttered, and the firefighters laughed. "Can we go now?" I asked Portia. She seemed to be hiding a smile, but she wasn't doing a very good job of it.

"Sure. Let's get back to Command."

"Wait! Daystar, Bill Johnson from the News. I just have a quick question."

I rolled my eyes and gestured to Portia to get on with getting us out of there.

"I've noticed since your fight against Maddoc that your powers seem different. With all due respect, you seem weaker," the reporter continued.

"Do I?" I asked sarcastically. Portia stood beside me with her hand on Darla's arm.

"Yes. I'm not the only one to have noticed. You don't punch the way you used to. It's like you're just throwing yourself at your opponents. The theory is that you sustained lasting damage against Maddoc and we're wondering, quite frankly, how you're supposed to protect us if you aren't one hundred percent."

Portia started to talk and I held my and up, and she want silent. "I actually do have something to say to that, Mr. Greenberg."

He held his phone out to capture my comment, and I raised each of my middle fingers at him, then raised them a little higher for emphasis, glaring through my mask.

I heard Portia sigh beside me, and she waved at the onlookers, then, in the next moment, she, Jenson, Amy, Darla, and I were standing in the detention facility at Command.

"Nice, Daystar. That was just lovely," she muttered when we reappeared.

"Oh, come on," I said when I realized where we were.

"Just for now. Until we figure this out and her parents get here," Portia said.

"Told you they were gonna lock me up," Darla told me.

"They are not."

"We're not," Portia said forcefully. "We're going to put you in one of these cells to talk to you while we try to figure this out. Okay?"

Darla just rolled her eyes. I was about to say something when Portia gave me a sharp look. I clamped my mouth shut. Even if I did feel like continuing to argue with her, what was there to say? "Oh, just let the cute little firestarter kid go. It'll be fine." Even I knew how ridiculous that sounded.

"You won't be alone in there, okay? One of us will stay with you until your parents get here. Okay?" I said to Darla, and she nodded.

I watched Portia and Amy take Darla toward the women's wing and was about to follow when Marie came running out of the men's wing.

"What's wrong?" I asked.

"That Maddoc asshole. He's got his hands loose. His feet are still secured, but none of us feel safe going in there to secure him. Portia's not answering her comm— "

"She's busy with something. What about Caine or Beta?"

"They just left for patrol. Caine was filling in for Monica today, so he just took off with Beta," she said.

I took a breath, trying to ease the way my stomach twisted. "Okay. I'll deal with it," I said.

I walked into the men's wing, Marie at my side. Three other prison guards were there, looking into the cell at the end of the hall. They were hanging back, looking more than a little worried.

"He's almost got one of his ankles free. He's angry, but he's also pretty pleased with himself right now," one of the men said. Bob, or Rob, or something like that. Low-level empath, which means he is able to pick up what others are feeling, but there's not a damn thing he can actually do with that information. It seems like a really frustrating power to have, and from what I'd heard, he'd been caught more than a few times drinking on the job.

I could hardly blame him. I'm not an empath in any way, shape, or form, but I sometimes want to drink on the job, too.

I walked past the guards, continuing down the corridor toward the cell on the end. The end cells are reinforced, for those with special powers. Maddoc inhabited it in this wing, and, when I'd been a prisoner, I'd inhabited the same cell in the women's wing. I kept walking, even though it felt like I was walking through mud. My stomach was churning, and all I really wanted to do was run.

My nightmares, when they weren't about things like my mother finding out what a fraud I am or being outed as a thief to the world, were nothing more than re-enactments of the last time I'd had to face Maddoc. Looking at him now, it all came slamming back to me. His enormous hands worked at the shackles around his ankle, and his bulging muscles strained under the effort. Veins stood out under his skin. He looked monstrous, and the cold, empty look in his eyes was one I wouldn't be forgetting any time soon.

He glanced up and saw me coming toward him. He paused in trying to free his ankle, and sat up straight, looking casual and at ease.

"Daystar," he said, loud enough that his voice echoed through the prison wing.

"Who turned his mic on?" I muttered.

"Rob did. He thought it would help us to hear what he was doing," Marie said.

"Did it?"

She shook her head. "It's not like we could do anything about it anyway."

"Stay back," I told her. "But be ready when I call you. Apparently, he's still pretty strong, even with the dampener on."

She nodded, and I kept moving forward, alone.

"You've been scarce here in the prison, Daystar. All your other teammates check in on us. Not you, though. Wonder why that is," he said, crossing his arms, watching me with a smirk on his face. "You're not scared, are you?"

I didn't answer. Because yes, to be honest, I was fucking terrified. I could feel his hands on my throat, strangling the life out of me. At the same time, I was enraged. I was missing parts of who I was supposed to be, because of him. I had nightmares every night, because of him. I still had headaches, and my body refused to work the way it should, especially when I was tired. All because of him.

"You want to play again, Daystar?" he taunted.

I didn't bother answering. I was thinking. Mostly, I was wondering if there was anyone else I could hand this particular shitty task off to. Since it seemed to be down to me, I had to figure out how to get him knocked out and restrained again without getting too close to him.

"Is Dani around?" I asked, pressing my comm.

"She is. What's going on down there, Daystar?" Jenson asked.

"Oh, nothing much. Just Maddoc, with two hands free, trying to break out of the rest of his shackles."

"Shit. Okay, I'll send Dani down to you. Do you want me to call David or Caine back in?"

"I got it. Just send Dani."

"Okay."

I turned and looked back at Maddoc, who was still sitting in the same position, looking smug.

"Too scared to come in, Daystar?"

"I just don't feel like dealing with your shit right now," I said.

"Right," he said with a smirk. "Come on in. Tie me down. Tell me what a bad boy I've been. You know you want to."

"Well, there goes my breakfast," I said in disgust.

"It's okay. We'll have plenty of time to play after my boss gets a hold of you."

"As if he has a chance in hell of doing that."

He smiled, an oily, slimy-looking smile. "I wouldn't write him off just yet. He's not like me. I get all impatient and ragey. Lose control. He's not like that. He won't make a mistake. But you will." Then he laughed. "You already have. You have no idea."

"What are you talking— " At that second, Maddoc kicked out, hard, and I heard the shackle on his leg snap. He was down to one, and that one was looking pretty bad.

Where the hell was Dani?

He was bent over pulling at the shackle around his ankle, and I glanced around.

"Daystar, his dampener is malfunctioning," Jenson said in my ear. Her normally calm voice sounded tense, stressed. "Do not go in there."

And then the final shackle snapped, and he gave a triumphant shout.

"Get someone else down here, now," I said. I ran forward, as fast as my clumsy legs would take me, and I met him at the door of his cell, which he was wrenching open from the inside. This. This is when the damage I sustained in my fight against him last time really hurt. I knew I was stronger than him, even when he wasn't dampened. The difference was, his reflexes were normal and mine were shit. A fight against Maddoc right now, an actual hand-to-hand fight, which was clearly what he wanted, just wasn't going to go my way no matter how bad I wanted to hurt him. I had to ignore my urge to try to make him pay. At least for now. This was about keeping him contained and away from everyone he could hurt if he got free.

I pushed hard against my side of the sliding door that separated his cell from the main corridor, trying to keep it pushed in the "closed" position, as he pushed in the opposite direction from his side. His face, up close through the shatterproof glass pane between us, turned red as he fought to open it.

"I am going to kill you when I get out of here," he shouted. "Fuck what the boss says."

I tried to ignore him, focusing all of my power on keeping the door closed. Every once in a while, he'd push harder and I'd lose some ground, the door slipping beneath my palms, but then I'd push harder and gain it back again.

"You'll die with my hands around your neck. Your eyes'll bulge, and your face'll turn purple— "

I tried to tune him out, even though his words made me flash back to that day. I'd tried, so many times, to insult or cajole myself into just "getting over it," to try to force myself to forget what it felt like. It's impossible to explain unless you've been there, unless you've felt yourself slipping away, how completely horrifying it is. And I've always prided myself on not being easy to scare, but those eternal moments, and the helplessness I felt as my lungs screamed for air and my chest exploded in pain, as my limbs went numb... I can't forget it.

"Your body lost control last time," he shouted. "Pissed yourself like a baby, you know that?" And then he laughed and pushed harder.

I felt the door start to creak, bending under the weight of the force we were putting on it. Reinforced steel, giving way under opposing sources of super-powered strength.

I heard footsteps behind me, running.

"We're here," I heard Jenson say.

"Dani?"

"I'm here."

"Do your thing. Knock this fucker out."

"It'll get you too, though," she said in a panicky tone.

"Better than him getting out and I'm starting to lose ground here. Do it!"

Dani went to the edge of the door, which was just starting to open as Maddoc pushed it open from his side. She opened her mouth wide, and everyone in the prison wing, myself included, was hit with a screeching blast of sound that felt like repeated stabs to the brain. I kept my eyes on Maddoc as I tried to ignore the agony. She'd been right next to his ear, ensuring that he got the worst of it, and he fell to the ground. I guess he was screaming, but I sure the hell wasn't able to hear it over Dani's eardrum shattering screech. He fell, hands to his ears, and I noted with some satisfaction that his ears were bleeding. As soon as he was down, I shoved the door open. Dani handed me a new dampener she'd brought with her as I walked past, and I nodded my thanks. I quickly fastened it around Maddoc's throat, clicking the latch on it shut tightly, which activated its dampening powers.

I gave Dani a weak thumbs-up, and the horrendous noise ended. She helped me get Maddoc (who was unconscious by this point, and, from the looks of it, most of those in the prison wing had succumbed as well) into a chair in the next cell over. We secured him with the manacles, and Jenson came back with a second dampener.

"Just in case," she said as she slipped it over his head and activated it. Her face was grim, angry, even. "How the hell could this happen?" she asked, and I wasn't sure if she was asking me or just venting out loud. I sure the hell didn't know how his dampener had managed to fail.

"Maybe it was faulty, or old, or something?" Dani said. Her voice was a little hoarse, which wasn't surprising after the damage she'd just done.

Jenson was staring fixedly at Maddoc. Then she walked over to Maddoc and took his original dampener off. It sat below the two thin metal rings we'd just put around his throat. She held it in her hands and inspected it closely.

"I'm going to see if Beta will take a look at this when he gets back. If it failed on its own, we need to know that so we can work on making sure it doesn't happen again. And if it failed thanks to someone messing with it…"

"I do not even want to think about that," I muttered.

"That makes two of us, but we need to consider it. We've never had one of these fail. Ever. Not even the one you had Marie re-size with her power when you tricked Alpha. That one's still working perfectly." Her brow was furrowed, her mouth a thin line.

"How would that even happen?" I asked. Dani leaned in, looking at the faulty tracker.

"I don't know. If someone disabled it remotely, figured out how to do that somehow, maybe? Or messed with the circuitry somehow. It's probably nothing. Probably just wore out or something. But I don't want to leave it to chance."

I nodded.

"What's going on with the girl you brought in?" Jenson asked.

"I don't know. Portia and Steel were walking her down to her cell last I saw."

"Oh. They had to leave. A call came in about some guy threatening to use his telepathy to destroy his enemies just after the Maddoc stuff started."

I shook my head and stalked toward the women's wing again. "I promised her she wouldn't be locked up alone," I said. "Damn it."

"You should rest or something," Jenson called after me. I didn't bother answering. I entered the women's detention wing again, peeking through the cell windows as I walked past them. I found Darla in one of the last cells on the left and hit the button to open the door. She wasn't manacled into the chair, thankfully. She was sitting, hunched into a little ball, at the far side of the cell.

"Hey."

"Hey," she said with a sniffle.

"They made a liar out of me. I promised you wouldn't be in here alone."

"They were about to go help you, I think, but then they said there was another bad guy they had to go after. Is it always like that here?"

I shrugged. "Some days are crazier than others." I sat down near her. Not too close, but close enough that she could talk without raising her voice. And, on the floor, she wouldn't have to crane her neck to look up at me. Hopefully, it would put her more at ease.

Like that was even possible.

"I'm gonna be stuck here forever now, aren't I? They can't just let me go, because what if I hurt someone? They'll be worried that I'll be the type of person they have to chase down." She closed her eyes, then rested her forehead on her knees.

"Look, the stuff you did was pretty minor, right?" I asked her. I mean, considering the damage she could have done, setting one house on fire when she was under stress wasn't all that serious. "Just sit tight for a while, and Steel will work something out so you can get out of here."

"Yeah?" she asked. Her eyes were still red from crying. Big brown eyes, full of fear and innocence. Had I ever been that young? I wondered. I doubted I'd ever been that innocent.

The one thing I did know is that having a kid here felt every kind of wrong. I remembered, way back when I'd first started working with Damian, that his dream had been to open a school for super powered kids, a place where they could feel like they belonged. Where they could feel safe.

It really sucked that he was a villain now. Because undoubtedly, if his little dream ever happened at this point, it would be to train a bunch of little super villains. Maybe it was something we should think about, though.

And as soon as I had the thought, I wanted to laugh. Yeah. Us. StrikeForce. We could barely manage ourselves, let alone training and being responsible for anyone else. We were a national, and probably an international, joke. Until very recently, the team had gotten its collective ass kicked almost every time it faced off against a villain. Now, our problem, more often than not, was that when a fight broke out, our enemies were usually whisked away by the teleporter they had on their side. So now the jokes were about how often we lose our villains.

So maybe we shouldn't be the ones to train the next generation of super heroes. But somebody should. Because then we wouldn't have to wonder what to do when an eleven year old girl sets a house on fire because she's stressed out over the crazy way her powers make her feel, which was what I guessed had happened.

"I know this is all kind of scary, probably," I continued. "You're not going to be here for long, Darla."

"I didn't mean to do it," she said in a tiny voice.

"I know you didn't," I said. I rested my back against the wall. "I made a big mess when I first got my powers. Way worse than what you did."

She looked at me, and I was relieved to have grabbed her interest. Anything was better than the terrified way she'd looked since we'd brought her in. "Yeah? What are your powers? I mean, I know you can fly."

I nodded. "I can fly. Super strength, super stamina."

"Were you scared when your powers showed up?" she asked, looking down.

"At first I was. It's scary. You feel all messed up inside, right? Like you're going to burst, and you don't know why."

She nodded, watching me.

"I felt like I forgot how to just do normal things, at first. I'd go to open a door, and I'd end up ripping the knob off, because my strength was more than I was used to. Sometimes, I'd open a door, and I'd end up taking it off of its hinges."

She laughed.

"And don't get me started on the first time I flew," I said, shaking my head.

"Tell me!"

So I told her. About how free I felt. And then about how I couldn't figure out how to land. I told it all, including the way I'd face-planted into the field behind a local school when I'd finally made it down. By the time it was done, she was laughing freely, and I couldn't help but laugh along.

"So how'd you manage to deal with it?"

I paused, shrugged. "The thing with the crazy, full feeling is that you have to use your powers. It's the only way to not feel like you're losing it. Obviously, you'll have to be careful about that. See if your parents can track down a big steel drum or one of those patio fire pits or something. Set fires there to release some of the pressure. The rest of it is just trying to be calm. I'm not good at that part." I told her about some of the calming exercises my doctor had given me after my injury from fighting Maddoc. I knew it was essentially meditation, but she didn't call it that, probably because she figured I'd brush it aside. At this point, though, I'd try just about anything to make the nightmares and anxiety go away.

"I destroyed our house," she said in a small voice, as if she'd just realized it.

I thought of the money sitting in the accounts Luther had helped me set up. Much more than I could ever use. More than StrikeForce would need for a while. I'd gotten a good amount of it before Jenson had frozen Alpha's accounts. I could keep the team afloat with some of it after we lost access to Alpha's money, which was bound to happen eventually. I had plans for a bit more of it, but there was still a lot left.

"We have a program… thing," I said. "We'll get you guys into another house. I'm pretty sure yours is not livable anymore."

"You'd do that?"

I nodded. "Um. When you get out, tell your parents about it, and once you guys find a good place, have them call me here."

She studied me. "Well, how much can we spend? I mean, what's the budget?"

I shook my head. "Tell you what. You guys find something in a neighborhood that works for you, and then tell me how much you need for it and we'll go from there."

"You're kidding."

"Well, I'm assuming you aren't going to go nuts. No gold toilets or any shit like that." I winced. "Excuse the language. Damn it."

"I've seen videos of you fighting. You say a lot worse than that," she said with a laugh.

"Shh. They're going to take away my official superhero badge if that gets out," I said with a laugh, and she joined in.

We were still laughing when the doors whooshed open, and Amy and Jenson stepped in. "I'm sorry we had to step out on you, Darla. Your mom and dad are here," Amy said. "I talked to them, and we're going to let you out of here now, but we're going to keep an eye on you. We need you to be careful, okay? I don't want you back here like this."

"Same here," she said.

She stood up and Jenson, Amy, and I walked her out to the lobby, where her parents, the woman we'd met at the scene and a graying man with the same kind eyes as his daughter, waited anxiously.

"We talked, we tried to give her some ideas for how to handle the stress," I said to her mother, who nodded, and kept her arms around her daughter. "As we've seen now, stress seems to trigger it, which is totally normal," I assured her. "So I gave her some things to practice for calming down, things my own doctor has me doing to help me deal with stress."

"Thank you so much," her father said.

"It was no problem at all. We were happy to help, and, more importantly, happy that we were able to talk to Darla before she started fearing her powers." I met Darla's eyes. "Your powers are nothing to fear, kiddo. They're you. One more facet of you, but you're still the person you've always been. Just... more."

She nodded, then reached out and hugged me for a moment before pulling away.

"Call if you need anything," I told her. "If you need to talk, or you're feeling stressed, or you just have questions or whatever. Call the StirkeForce line, and if you want to talk to me, they'll put you through to me or have me call you back. Or if you want to talk to Steel or Portia or Jenson or whoever. And about the other thing we talked about."

"I can really do that?"

"You really can. Don't hesitate to call if you want. Okay?"

After a few more moments of chatting, Darla and her parents left. Jenson and I watched them walk out, past the guards.

"You were very good with her," Jenson said quietly. I shrugged. She nudged me with her elbow. "That's the Jolene I know is in there. That's the Daystar I believe in. You're holding onto the thief thing, and I think you don't even know why anymore, do you?" she asked, and I didn't answer. "You're so much more. I've seen you grow into who you are, bit by bit over the last few weeks. You need to let that old crap go. Be the hero everyone other than you already knows you to be."

"It's easy for you to say that," I pointed out. "Look at you. Former soldier, police officer. I bet you started as a safety patrol kid in elementary school or some shit like that, didn't you?"

Jenson rolled her eyes and started walking back toward the elevator.

"You did, didn't you?" I asked with a laugh.

"For your information, my first position was lunch room helper."

"Oh, sorry," I said. "Did you have a badge?" I teased.

"You bet I did," she answered.

"See?"

"See what?"

"You were born to be the hero. You've probably never done a stupid thing in your entire life. You're the most sickeningly together person I've ever known, Jenson."

"I'll take that as a compliment."

"Ugh."

Jenson laughed. "I was a good girl growing up. And I stuck to the straight and narrow mainly because my parents put the fear of God in me at an early age. They were strict, and I never stepped a toe out of line."

I watched her. Jenson never talks much about herself. She's probably my closest friend on the team, with Caine coming in a close second, probably, but I know almost nothing about her.

"But I've done stupid things. Made mistakes," she said with a small nod. "There are things I've done that I'd love to go back and undo, but I can't. All I can do is keep moving forward and trying to be the best version of myself I can be."

"The best version of yourself," I murmured. "That sounds like you're pretending, or acting, or something."

She shrugged. "Sometimes. Sometimes, all I want to do is haul off and smack some of the people we work with, not to mention the ones we try to apprehend. Sometimes, all I want to do is walk away, take my savings and find a nice little tropical island somewhere where nobody needs me to do anything for them."

"You could do that," I said.

"I could," she agreed. "I definitely could. But that's not the person I'm trying to be. It's not the version of myself that I'm working toward. You're right about me. I want to at least try to be a hero. I want to be the type of person people know they can count on. That's not the kind of person who runs off when they know they're needed."

The elevator doors opened on our floor, and Jenson and I walked down the corridor toward where our suites were located.

"I mean, you must have had bigger dreams for yourself once upon a time," she said. "No little kid grows up saying 'I want to be a thief when I grow up!'"

"I did."

"You are so full of shit, Faraday," Jenson said. "Wishing you and your mom had more money is not the same as saying that you dreamed of being a person who stole stuff from other people."

We reached my door and I pressed my thumb to the keypad. "You're right," I said.

"Of course. So what did you want to be when you grew up?" she asked.

"A space pirate."

Jenson shook her head and gave me an irritated look that I couldn't help laughing at. "You are the worst," she said.

"I know." I grinned at her.

"Seriously. Just the worst." She started walking across the hall toward her suite.

"And you're always hanging out with me, so what does that make you?" I shot back, still grinning.

She turned to look back at me after getting her door open. "I represent the better angels of your nature. Good night. Try not to steal anything."

I gave her a one finger salute, which she returned, and then I closed my door and peeled off my uniform as I made my way to my bedroom. I wanted salty, crunchy snacks and something to watch that had nothing to do with heroes or villains or anything even remotely resembling my life.

I ended up settling for potato chips and old reruns of the Dukes of Hazzard. I wondered, for a second, what kind of crap Connor liked do do in his down time, and then I remembered that it really wasn't worth thinking about. I may be a mess, but even I know that some things are more trouble than I know how to handle. And Connor was definitely one of them.

Almost as if on cue, my phone rang. And I knew after the first ring who it was. I looked at my phone, letting it ring. When it finally stopped, I turned my attention back to the television without really seeing it. A couple of minutes later, my phone beeped. Voice mail.

I took a deep breath and picked it up to listen to the message.

"Hey, Jolene." His hoarse growl was immediately recognizable. "I'm back around, so I was wondering if you wanted to get together. I really want to see you. I feel like things went in a bad direction last time." He paused, and it was silent for a couple seconds. "Let's just try again, huh? You know nobody will ever want you the way I do, right? You have to know that. You're all I think about." There was another pause. "And if anyone ever did try to convince you to choose them over me, I guess we'd see just how much of a bad guy I still am, eh?" A chill went up my spine at the menace in his tone. "I'll call again. I know you're too fuckin' stubborn to call me back. You really should answer next time. We need to work this out and I'm not a patient man. Bye, sweetheart."

The message ended, and I sat looking at my phone. He was starting to look like one of those Lifetime movies Mama used to watch when I was a teenager, about the perfect guy who ends up being a stalker. And I always watched those movies thinking "how dumb is this chick? Doesn't she see what a jerk he is?" Guess the joke's on me. It was just my luck that not only was he kind of turning out to be a class A jerk, but of course he was super-powered as well. When I mess up, clearly I mess up big.

I shook my head, determined not to let myself obsess over it. I was tired of thinking about Connor and what he'd told me and trying to decide what I should do about it, if anything. He was clearly not doing his old shit anymore, on the news every few days saving one person or another. He'd moved on, but I still couldn't reconcile what I'd seen when I'd looked into Raider with what I saw every day on the news. And then there was this latest stalkery bullshit.

I shoved the thoughts aside, but, unfortunately, the next place they went was to my face-off against Maddoc. His threats. And unlike Connor, Maddoc did actually scare me. It's not a feeling I'm all that used to, and it pisses me off to feel it at all. I remembered what Jenson had told me and I picked my phone back up again and messaged Caine.

"Hey. Someone told me I should learn wrestling moves to make up for how shit my punches are now. Jenson said maybe you can help?" I texted to him.

A few seconds later, an answer appeared on my screen. "I can do that. After our shift tomorrow?"

"Gotta do some looking around with Jenson and Amy tomorrow for Death. Afternoon?"

A couple seconds later, "Sure. Meet you in the training room around three?"

I thanked him, then set my phone down, and it beeped again. I picked it back up.

"Night, Jo," Caine had texted. "Try not to hurt me too bad tomorrow."

I laughed a little, picturing my enormous partner, and messaged back. "I'll try not to. Night."

Action. Doing stuff. I could do that. All of this sitting around and thinking was enough to make me crazy.

# CHAPTER SIX

I spent the morning checking out a couple of Dr. Death's favorite haunts with Jenson and Amy, but it came to nothing. Between the complete waste of time of the morning and my crappy dreams the night before, I was more than ready to spend some time sparring with Caine. I walked into the gym to find him already there, dressed in dark gray sweats and a white t-shirt.

"You feeling okay?" he asked in greeting. "How are your ribs after the other night?"

"They're all right. I'm fine."

"Jolene."

"Ryan," I said, mimicking his deep voice. I realized it was the first time I'd actually called him by anything other than his code name. It suited him. And I felt another of those little walls between myself and my team members come tumbling down. These people were slowly but surely becoming more than just a bunch of randoms I had to work with every day. It was weird being part of a team. And the even weirder thing was that I kind of liked it.

He grinned at me then, a flash of perfect white teeth, and we stood there for a couple of seconds. He shook his head a little and said, "I heard about your thing yesterday with Maddoc. I guess that's why you asked about doing this now?"

I nodded. "That, and I'm still frustrated that Death slipped away from me again. Clearly I need to do better."

"You did an amazing job with the transporter and Damian and everything the other night. Even if you did give me a heart attack when you disappeared from the museum like that. I hate that shit. I was supposed to be out there with you."

"I just wanted to make sure she didn't slip away again."

"Yeah, well you managed that. What if she'd ended up taking you to their headquarters or something like that, where they'd had more backup?"

"I would have flown away. And then we would have known exactly where to find the bitches."

He crossed his arms over his chest and watched me. "You have an answer for everything don't you?"

"Of course," I said.

"I'll find some way to trip you up eventually," he said.

"We'll see. Are we going to do this or yak all day, because if I wanted to do that, I'd hang out with the assholes in the prison wing."

He laughed and waved me toward the left side of the room, where he'd put a few mats on the floor.

"Okay. The best way to learn these is to have them done to you first so you know what it's supposed to feel like," he said. "We're going to focus mostly on moves that start with your opponent down, since, I think, from what you said before, that the plan is to stun them by flying into them with all of your weight and knocking them down, then using the wrestling moves to subdue them, right?"

"Right."

"Okay. Down on the mat then, on your stomach, like I just knocked you down."

I nodded and lowered myself to the mat.

"Are you sure your ribs are okay?"

"Yeah."

"I don't want to hurt you."

"If you don't get going, you're going to be the one hurting," I warned him sweetly.

"Well, you're such a delicate little flower," he teased.

"Ryan."

"Fine." He stepped over me, one foot on either side of my hips, and then I felt him crouch behind me. "So this move is really good if you're dealing with someone who's probably going to regain their balance pretty quickly and you definitely want to subdue them fast. It's not pretty or delicate. Brute force."

I nodded. He rested one knee on my lower back and put weight on it, then he put both hands on my chin, pressed against my throat.

I felt myself starting to panic. I stiffened.

"Jolene. Relax," he said.

My breathing got more rapid, and he lowered his hands to my neck completely. I tried to scramble away from him, but he kept his knee pressed lightly into my back. "Calm down," he said gently. He massaged my throat gently with warm, firm hands. "Breathe. You're safe. I'm here, and you're a hell of a lot scarier than I am."

I felt myself start hyperventilating, and he got off of me with a muttered "shit." Ryan pulled me up so I was sitting, then he left for a second and came back with a bottle of water. I guzzled it and tried to calm my breathing, the knot in my stomach. "I'm sorry," he said.

"You didn't do anything."

"I should have stopped right away."

"No. If I'd wanted you to, I would have told you so. I need to get over this shit," I said angrily. "Again, and I'll try not to freak out."

"You're sure?"

I nodded and got back on my stomach. A few seconds later, I felt him settle his knee into my lower back again.

"I'm putting my hands on your chin now," he said quietly, and I nodded. He placed his hands back on my chin, and I could feel myself starting to panic a little but I focused on my breath, on breathing through the panic. "So this one works because you use your body weight on their lower back, which hurts like a bitch. I'm not putting my full weight down, because I'm balancing on my other leg. If you were doing this, you'd put all your weight on the leg that's resting on your opponent's back."

"Okay," I said.

"Then you rest their arms over your thighs, so they can't use their arms to leverage themselves back up. Take control away from them, right? That's not enough, in and of itself to subdue someone, though. That's what you use your hands for. While your knee is planted in their back, pull their chin back and up." He started pulling my chin up, back. It was majorly uncomfortable, and would have been excruciating if he'd been resting all his weight on me. As it was, I already felt like I would crack in half. He released me.

"Your turn to try it," he said. He got face down on the mat, and when I stood over him, he told me to put all of my weight down, the way I was supposed to.

"Don't be stupid. I'll hurt you."

"Right now the only thing you're hurting is my ego. Just do it, Jolene. I'm a hell of a lot bigger than you, and you're not the only one here who can hold their own in a fight."

"Fine." I pressed my knee into his back, letting all of my weight rest there.

"Okay. Do it. Put your weight on it," he said.

"I am!"

"You sure?"

"I'm sure."

"Okay. Then do the rest of it."

I put my hands under his chin, and he adjusted my hands so they were in the best position, then I pulled his arms up over my thighs, locking them back so he wouldn't be able to use his hands, and I pulled up and back, the way he told me to.

"Good," he said, and I let him go. "Again."

I did it a few more times, and then he stood up. "Okay. Come at me the way you'd come at an enemy. Knock my ass down and then do that hold, just like we practiced. The key will be getting fast at it."

"You want me to just bash into you at full strength?" I asked him unsurely.

Ryan grinned. "Don't worry. You're not going to break me."

"I might."

"Doubt it. You should totally try though and see what happens."

I backed up. "Just remember that this was your idea."

He nodded and gestured for me to come at him. I rose into the air, reared up, and flew at full speed toward him. I hit Ryan at full strength and he flew across the mats, landing in a heap at the end of the sparring area. I flew over to him, settled myself onto his back, and was starting to pull at his arms when he started fighting back, refusing to let me get a good grip on his arms, then eventually flipping me over and pulling my arm, hard, behind my back.

"You need to be faster," he said. "Again."

We did it a few more times, and I failed to get him down every time.

"Oh, come the fuck on," I said after the fifth time. "This isn't even fair. Most of the assholes I have to fight aren't as big as you are."

"I'm just gonna bask for a while in having a woman tell me how big I am," he said with a grin.

I crossed my arms and glared at him.

"Wasn't it like, what? Ten minutes ago that you were worried about hurting me?" he asked, walking past me to grab another bottle of water from the cooler.

"I didn't know you were that strong," I muttered.

"Do it again," he said after gulping down the entire bottle of water.

"How about showing me something else?"

"This is the most effective one for what you're talking about."

"Something else," I repeated, and he shook his head.

"Fine." He got behind me. "This one works a couple of ways. If you manage to sneak up on someone from behind, you can subdue them with this from a standing position. And if you get them down, you can still do it, with the added advantage that you can put your weight on them if you really need to. " He stepped close behind me, put his arms under mine, then bent his elbows, pulling my arms and shoulder blades back. He joined his hands behind my head, and, hard as I tried. I couldn't get out of it.

"This is a basic nelson hold," he told me. "You can make it hurt more if you push their head forward more." He put a little more pressure on the back of my head, and I felt the tension along my neck, back, and shoulders. "Try again to get out of it."

I did. I tried. I tried bucking him off of me, slithering out of his hold, and none of it worked.

"Fuck," I muttered, and he let go.

"See? It's a good one, right?"

I nodded. "And if they're down?" I asked.

"Same general idea." He gestured to the mat, and I got down on my stomach. He straddled my back, rather than resting his weight on me, and did the same hold, pulling me back hard, and I struggled against him. In my struggling against him, I lifted my backside up and into him. I heard Ryan groan, and then he let go of me abruptly and moved away.

"That's good for today," he said hoarsely.

"Did I hurt you?"

"Nope." He started walking toward the door.

"What? So that's it?"

"I have stuff I need to do and I think you got it."

"You were just saying that I'm not fast enough!"

I watched as he let his head fall back and looked up at the ceiling like he was trying to gather his patience or something.

"You did all right," he finally said.

"I did not," I said irritably.

"You did," he insisted, turning around to look at me. "If you want to keep working, maybe we should work on your punches for a while."

"Why? That's pointless."

"Did this help? Did it make you feel less restless and on edge? Less full?" I watched him. I remembered telling him, when we first started as partners, about how the fact that it felt like I had all this energy built up with nowhere to put it was almost as bad as being weaker since the fight against Maddoc.

"No," I said quietly.

"Okay. So this is good in that it gives you another tool, another type of attack. They probably won't expect that from you, which is good."

"So why are you going on about punching then? I'm useless. My speed is fucked, my coordination is non-existent."

He didn't answer for a minute. "You said it yourself: the weird energy, that full feeling, like what you felt when you first got powers and didn't know what to do with them... it's back, right? And this isn't helping it."

I nodded.

"And it's not a good feeling, right? Makes it hard to concentrate. Hard to keep your head straight."

"Yeah."

"Okay. I have this theory, and Dr. Ali shares it, that our powers or abilities or whatever you want to call them want to be used. You can't use your power the way you did originally."

"Yeah. Thanks for mentioning that again," I said, crossing my arms.

He gave me an impatient look. "You're missing the point. Let's just try it. Maybe you just need to bust through, maybe if you try to use it enough, your power will find a way to compensate for what you lost. Give you extra speed for make up for it, or something." I just watched him. "It's worth a try, right?"

"We should just go back to wrestling," I said.

He looked away. "I've had enough of that for today. But if you want to do some punching, I'm here."

I threw my hands up in defeat. "Fine. Let's do punching."

Ryan put punching pads on both of his hands, held them up, and gestured for me to start. I started punching, jabbing at the pads. It was embarrassing. It felt like trying to punch through water, except that the water is rushing at you, weighing you down, slowing you down, and while you eventually make it through, just getting there wears you out completely. After a few minutes, I stopped and snarled in disgust.

"This is useless," I said.

"Keep hitting," he said, glaring at me over the punching pads as he held them up.

"We're done."

"I had no idea you were such a quitter, Faraday," Ryan taunted. "What, you only bother showing a little effort when you're trying to rob people?"

I flipped him the bird, and he kept going.

"Or maybe you're just too scared to keep going. It's hard not measuring up, isn't it?"

"Oh, fuck off," I muttered. I turned like I was going to walk away.

"Takes you back, huh? Like you never left the trailer park at all. Like you're every single thing the people who were jerks to you ever said you were."

"Shut up," I muttered.

"Make me, Faraday," he said, jutting his chin at me. I turned again and started walking.

"So that's it? Throw in the towel? Let Dr. Death and his assholes win? Because without you, this team doesn't have a chance in hell of catching him, and you know it."

"Why is that my fucking problem?" I yelled.

"Oh, I don't know. Because he's the one that set his fucking rabid dog on you so you'd stop making trouble for him. But you're right. Walk away. Let it be someone else's problem. You never asked to be a hero. Maybe you're not."

I snarled and launched toward him, pulling my hand back to punch. Before I even had a chance to try to start moving my fist forward, he flew back into the wall, like a strong gust of wind or something had swept him away.

I stared, and he picked himself up and readjusted the punching pads.

"What the hell was that?" I asked him.

"Pretty sure that was your power finding a way to work around what Maddoc did to you. Now are you going to work with it, or are you going to run away?"

"I'm not running," I said, circling him.

He held his hands up, the punching pads out toward me. "Show me."

I did. It was hit or miss, literally, for a while, but every once in a while, I'd make it happen again, and he'd go flying across the mats.

"It seems like I have to make sure I'm focusing pretty hard to make it happen," I said, out of breath once Ryan finally called a break. He nodded, and I passed the bottle of water I'd been sipping from over to him. He gulped some down, then handed it back.

"I bet it'll get easier the more you do it. From what I felt, you're gonna do some damage with that." We were sitting side by side on the bench near the area where we'd been sparring. I bumped my shoulder into his arm, and he bumped me back.

"Thanks for sticking with me even after I went all crab ass on you."

"I'm just glad it actually seems to be something that'll work." After a few minutes, we got up and headed toward the elevator.

"Are you on tonight?" he asked me, and I shook my head.

"No, but we're doing this girls' night out thing," I said with a grimace.

Ryan laughed. "Oh, right. You sound pretty excited about it."

"I like hanging out with them and all that. I just don't like the going out part." I glanced up at him. "How much do you know about Killjoy?" I asked him quietly. I didn't even know why, other than the fact that he'd been the one person on the team who hadn't outright hated him.

He shrugged and I thought he wouldn't answer. "I don't know anything. Less than you, for sure, I'm guessing. All I really know is that Alpha can't stand him, and Alpha's a prick. So I guess it's a whole 'enemy of my enemy' thing. I liked watching him make Alpha and Nightbane look like idiots." He watched me. "Alpha's not exactly my favorite person, so it was all I needed to know," he finally said. "Why?"

I shrugged.

"Is that getting serious? You and him?"

I shook my head. "I don't think so."

"Do you want it to?"

"I don't know," I said. What I really wanted to ask him was what he thought of the original Raider, because I'd come across photos of a fight between him and Raider from about eight years ago, not long after the first Confluence, when powers first started popping up. Ryan had already been on StrikeForce at the time, though I knew that how he came to be on StrikeForce was a little murky. Like me, he hadn't ended up on the team entirely by choice.

We ended up not saying anything else, and, after a moment, the doors opened on my floor and I gave him a small nod as I left the elevator. Now I had to clean up and get myself ready for a fun night of not working.

I seriously was sure that I didn't even know how.


At a little after nine, once Portia and Dani had finished their shift and everyone had had a chance to clean up and change, a group of us loaded up into cars in the parking garage. Jenson, Monica, and I ended up riding with Amy in one car, while Portia, Chance, Toxxin, and Marie rode in the other.

The weirdest thing was seeing them all dressed up and with make up on and their hair done. Usually, if we weren't walking around in our uniforms, we were in sweats or pajamas. Except for Jenson. Jenson always dressed like she was ready for a job interview or something.

We ended up deciding on Mexican, and we ended up at one of the big restaurants in the Mexicantown neighborhood of Detroit. Once we were seated and had drinks, the table got pretty quiet as we all sat around, kind of looking at everyone else in the restaurant and not knowing what to say if we weren't talking about work.

"We are an utter bunch of dorks," Amy finally said, and the rest of us laughed. "Okay, here's something. Slowly but surely, I'm noticing that people are starting to call other team members by their actual name. I notice Jenson and Jolene calling Beta 'David.' And you all have known our names," she said, indicating herself, Monica, and Dani, " from the start. And Jolene's of course," she added. "I think we all realize we're here as much because we need to get better at working together as because we needed a night out. So, I don't know. Maybe that's something we can start with."

"Only if you want to, though," I said. "Because to be honest, I probably wouldn't have given anyone my actual name if I'd ever had a choice in the matter."

"Good point," Amy said.

"Well. I'm fine with that," Toxxin said. "I'm Ariana. I'm twenty-nine. I joined up when I was nineteen. At first, because I wanted to be there, and later, I was there because I had to be." Toxxin... Ariana, had been the other one, besides Caine on the original team, who Alpha had kept collared. The reasons why were apparently things only a few people knew, and they weren't talking about them. Not yet, anyway. "I spent nine years under his thumb," she said quietly. "While some of the people at this table, who could have tried to do something at the time, sat around with their heads up their asses." I noticed Portia, especially, looking uncomfortable, but Jenson wasn't looking all that confident just then, either. "I'm here because I want to be part of something good, and I think we can be that. But don't expect me to feel all chummy with everyone. Not just yet. I need a little time."

I was watching Ariana as she spoke, and she glanced up and met my eyes. "Of course, if Jolene ever has to walk through the nine levels of hell, I'll volunteer for the trip," she said with a grin, and I smiled back.

Portia cleared her throat. "And I'm sorry about that. All of it," she said to Ariana, who just gave a small nod in response. "My name actually is Portia. I liked the fact that it matched up so well with what I do," she said with a shrug. "And I don't have anyone I need to protect, so there was no reason to change it. Portia Jones," she said. "I'm thirty-four. Joined up when I was twenty-four, and stayed because I love doing what I do. I just wish I'd been a little stronger along the way," she said, glancing at Ariana.

Chance was sitting next to Portia. She looked around. "I'm going to stay with the option of keeping my name to myself," she said quietly.

Monica was about to say something to argue with her, and I shook my head. She clamped her mouth shut. I wasn't going to push Chance. And I also knew there wasn't a chance in hell Jenson would be telling us anything. And sure enough, when our little group started looking at Jenson expectantly, she sat there sipping her drink as if she had no idea what they expected from her. After the silence went on for a while, she gave us an exasperated look. "I'm keeping it to myself. Obviously."

"So everyone except you two shared their names. What makes you so special?" Monica asked.

"And Caine. Nobody knows Caine's real name," Jenson said, and I tried to keep my expression from giving away my surprise. "I mean, Portia, you were his partner for over five years, right? Did he tell you?" Jenson pressed.

Portia shook his head. "I have a feeling that's one of those things that's going to stay a mystery." She glanced at me. "He hasn't told you, has he, Jolene?"

I shook my head.

"So, there we go. A few of us have elected, for whatever reasons, to keep our names to ourselves. It doesn't mean I like you all any less, though," Jenson said. Things seemed to have gotten tense again, where we seemed to have been making some headway before. Finally, our food came, and we managed some halting conversation while we ate. Most of it was along the lines of "hey, this is really good!" but I guess it was a start.

We were on to dessert when Portia asked, "so what are we doing next?"

"Going home?" I asked hopefully, and Jenson gave me an exasperated look.

"No," she said, and I smiled sweetly.

"We could go to a movie. I know you all were talking about gambling, but I don't have any money to gamble with," Monica said.

"I don't want to go to the casino either," I said.

"Movies?" Portia asked, and we all gave kind of noncommittal shrugs.

Jenson took a last bite of her flan and looked around. "I know what we should do."

"What?" I asked, just kind of knowing I would hate it.

"Ice skating. I've never skated at Campus Martius. We should go!"

I was about to protest, but Portia, Ariana, and Amy all started excitedly chattering about going, and even Monica and Chance looked interested. Marie and I were the only ones less than thrilled with the idea, but in the end we both decided to go with it. It would be better than the casino, anyway.

We drove through downtown to Campus Martius, rented some skates and then we all got out onto the ice. Mostly, it ended up that Marie, Monica, Amy, and I ended up hugging the railing for dear life and inching around the rink while Jenson and the rest of them glided past us. I fell on my ass a handful of times, but by the time we decided to call it a night, all of us were laughing and a lot less awkward together. As we drove back, I was relieved that it was over, but even I had to admit that we'd needed it. Anything that made us less of a mess was a good thing

When we pulled back into the garage at Command, we all streamed toward the elevators, Monica and Dani with their arms around each other's waists, murmuring quietly together, the rest of us tired but probably more relaxed than we'd been since I'd been on the team.

We were on the elevator heading up to our suites for the night, and everyone was in a good mood, tired but chatty, and Jenson and I exchanged a look.

"Good idea, Jenson," I admitted, and she grinned. Just then, my comm crackled.

"Hey, you're back," David said in my ear. "I found some stuff. Do you want to come down here? Or wait til tomorrow?"

I touched my comm. "I'll be there. I'll bring Jenson."

The elevator stopped on our floor, and everyone but me and Jenson got off. I hit the button to go back down, and Jenson gave me a questioning look.

"David said he found something, I'm guessing in those files you were having him working on. I said we'd go down and take a look."

She nodded, and we got off the elevator and headed into David's lab.

# CHAPTER SEVEN

Jenson and I walked through the double doors into David's work space. He was hunched over his keyboard, looking at the monitor. Reading something, I supposed. Ryan was standing nearby, leaning back against one of the work tables that David always had a bunch of parts and papers piled up on. He had his arms crossed over his chest and a stony expression on his face. I met his eyes for a moment, and his expression didn't change.

"Let's take a look at what you found," Jenson said, and David raised his head and watched us walk the rest of the way toward them. He stood up and motioned to his chair, and I took it while Jenson dragged one over from another part of the lab. I sat down, nodding my thanks, and he tapped the display a few times, opening a variety of documents.

"Okay. This first one is the first time we see any mention of what it is they're planning to do with the samples," he said, and I leaned forward and started reading.

"An injection?" I asked after a couple of minutes of reading.

"Yeah."

I read some more. "So… they were using the samples to try to… what? Create something that would give ordinary people powers?"

"Seems like it. And it fits with what we knew Dr. Death was already working on, with that mess Mayhem created in Midtown."

I nodded. Dr. Death and Mayhem had built a machine that released a gas that was supposed to turn anyone who breathed it in into a powered person. Something had gone horribly wrong, and we'd ended up with almost three dozen corpses. It was the reason Alpha had finally had no choice but to let me out after Mayhem.

"Why, though?" I said, still scanning through the document.

"From this next document," David said, clicking over to another one, "it looks like the ultimate goal is to create a super powered army under the control of what they're calling 'The Conclave.'"

I leaned forward and read. "They're fucking crazy," I murmured as my stomach twisted. "I mean… creation of a super powered army, wresting control of international governments, creating a world-wide force under their command. This is super whack-job world domination shit right here."

"I know," David said. "Uh. From this other one, I guess Alpha must have asked his contact the same question. Mostly, he wanted to know what was in it for him, because, you know: Alpha," he said.

"Of course," I agreed.

"But besides that, he asked what the endgame is. And this was his contact's response." He pulled up another document and I started reading.

"So Alpha is promised more money than he could ever imagine, along with exclusive contracts to keep providing 'The Conclave' with more varied samples and a position of importance in their new little super villain club." I read some more. "'To bring a lasting peace to the world.' Is he serious with this bullshit?"

"Villains always say crap like that," Jenson muttered. "What it means, of course, is ultimate control and the ability to do whatever they want, however they want it, without having to sneak around or have someone like StrikeForce or any of the other cities' forces on their backs."

"It's like in *The Godfather*, when Michael wanted to make the family legitimate, but he had to do all of this bad shit to get there," I said, still reading. "But then you realize in the end that it was all pretty words and while he may have started out okay, he ultimately loved power more than anything or anyone else."

"Is everything a movie reference with you?" Jenson asked with a laugh.

"You can relate any important topic to a movie," I said. "Or it's ultimately not that important." I read some more. "He mentions me here. Alpha," I clarified.

"Yeah, I saw that," David said. "It looks like that was right after you crashed into our prison wing," he added, pointing at the metadata for the document. "It looks like there was some heavy back and forth negotiating over your sample, with Alpha wanting a higher price for it. His contact finally agrees to it here," he said, pointing at another document, "but then there's a bit of back and forth because they guy's pissed that Alpha's taking so long to get your sample."

"I'm guessing I'm the 'blond bitch' mentioned here," I said, scanning through the document. "Those are some high numbers they're throwing around there," I said, noting the price Alpha had finally accepted as payment once he got a sample of my blood.

A thought struck me, and I looked over at Jenson in alarm. "When I was in the hospital, they would have taken blood," I said.

"He wasn't able to do anything with it then, though. Caine and I had him scared, and he didn't leave his office.

And, that last email where the contact is mad that he doesn't have your sample yet... look at the date." I did. It was three weeks after my fight against Maddoc. I realized with a start, that it was from the day we'd staged our little coup and locked Alpha and his people up. I felt a knot release in my stomach.

"Okay. Well that's a relief, as long as nothing changed between the time this was sent and when we took control."

"So... I mean, I think we can safely assume this is Dr. Death, right?" David asked, and Jenson and I both nodded. "So, we have evidence here now that he was negotiating with a super villain to sell him samples of blood for his little science experiment, without our permission and with ill intent. If this isn't enough for the international tribunal to take him off our hands, lock him up, and throw away the key, I don't know what is."

"I agree," Jenson said. Then she smiled at David. "Amazing job. These files drove me nuts for so long. And now we finally have something more concrete."

"Yeah, that's all great, and I'm glad Jolene's blood isn't out there, but mine is. So's yours," Ryan said to Jenson and David. "And Dr. Death is apparently working on some injection to give others our powers, or a mix of them, or all of them for all we know. What are we gonna do about that part of it?"

"We'll catch him," I said, meeting his eyes. He shook his head and stormed out of the lab. I quickly thanked David and Jenson, then followed him out.

"Hey," I said as he was getting onto the elevator. He held the door open for me, and I got on with him. "It'll be okay. We'll catch him and — "

"Despite the fact that we haven't managed that yet, there's something else," Ryan said.

"I know, he might have used the samples already. And if he has we'll deal with that when— "

"No."

"No, we won't deal with it?" I asked him.

He turned to me, looking down at me. He was pissed, and I've never seen him actually pissed before. You had the sense that he was barely containing his anger, that the second he could, he'd let it go and somebody would have a really, really bad day. "No. The issue is this, partner: you knew this shit had happened. For, what? A week or so now? Maybe longer? You knew Alpha took my blood, and you kept it from me."

I opened my mouth, then closed it again. "I didn't know what he was doing with it, or even if it had gone through at all. I didn't see any point in telling anyone until they uncovered more."

"You didn't see any point in telling me that my blood had been taken from me under false pretenses, and that he was negotiating money for it? Are you kidding me?"

"Ryan," I began, and he shook his head.

"I thought you'd be different from them, Jo. I thought you understood what it was to have your choices taken from you."

"I do." He looked away, and I shook my head. "I'm sorry," I said quietly. "It was wrong not to tell you. And it says a lot about my screwy sense of ethics, but I honestly didn't even think of telling you. It just never crossed my mind, because I was just focusing on the hope that they'd find out more."

The elevator stopped on my floor and I stepped off, and, to my surprise, so did he. I looked up at him, and he started walking toward my suite.

"We're gonna talk about this. And you're gonna tell me everything you know so far about Dr. Death and these samples." He looked down at me. "Right?"

"Right." I unlocked my door and we stepped into my suite, then sat down at the little dining table, and I told him everything we'd uncovered so far while he sat there in stony silence. When I was done, he got up and left without a word.

It takes a lot to make me feel like a jerk. Ryan managed to do it without uttering a word. That, or I was getting soft, I thought as I fell into bed. We had a patrol shift in a couple of hours.

"That should be fun," I muttered as I fell into bed and closed my eyes. Bet he was regretting telling me his real name now, I thought as I pulled the blankets up over my head.

# CHAPTER EIGHT

After making it through a tense and entirely silent patrol shift with Ryan, I walked up the front walk of the house I'd bought for Mama, taking a good look as I did. I could see why she liked it so much. Cute Craftsman bungalow with a front porch that spanned the whole front of the house. It was painted a happy yellow, which was my mom's favorite color. The front yard had an enormous maple tree, and I could imagine how pretty it would look in spring and summer, when everything was green. Or in fall, with red and orange leaves. I smiled to myself. I could absolutely see Mama living here, in this nice little neighborhood with the grocery store in walking distance, a bakery just a few blocks away. She'd be pissed at me for buying it, but she'd fall in love with it. I knew that much about Mama. She'd chide me every chance she got, but she'd be grateful.

I stomped up the wood front steps and unlocked the front door. I turned on lights in some of the first floor rooms, since it was so dreary outside. I walked through the rooms, looking around, noting things I wanted fixed.

Honestly, I didn't have very high hopes for this contractor, carpenter, whatever. The last one hadn't shown up at all, which pissed me off doubly since I'd had to take David's early morning patrol shift to work it in. And the one before that had wanted to rip everything out and start over with new drywall, new floors, new everything. What's the point of buying an old house and putting all new shit in it? My mother would hate that.

I could picture Mama having her coffee in the little breakfast nook in the kitchen. Maybe setting up her old sewing machine in one of the first floor bedrooms. She loved to sew, but she always had to dig her sewing machine and other stuff out of our storage unit and then set up on the dining room table in our trailer when she wanted to work on a project, which meant that she didn't bother very often anymore. When I was a kid, before we lost our first house, she used to sew all the time.

I smiled to myself. I could not wait to walk her into this house. I could picture it all fixed up, just waiting for Mama. Hopefully the repairs wouldn't take too long.

I heard a knock on the front door and I walked through the dining and living rooms. A man was standing on the front porch. Much younger than the first contractor I'd talked to, probably in his mid thirties or so. He had dark hair, a little wavy and probably overdue for a trim. Dark eyebrows and a bit of dark scruff on his jawline. He wore jeans and a navy blue button-down shirt.

"Hi. Justin Rhys," he said when I came to the door. I opened it and waved him in.

"Jolene Faraday," I said, sticking my hand out awkwardly. He took it and shook my hand. "Thanks for coming by."

"Happy to do it. This is a great house," he said, looking around.

I nodded. "It is. I just bought it. It's for my mother, actually."

"Nice daughter," he murmured, glancing at me with a smile before continuing to look around. He had brown eyes, with just a hint of smile lines beginning to form at the corners. I looked away.

"Well, I figured it was the least I could do after what a little shit I was when I was a kid."

"Now that you're totally reformed, right?" he asked, grinning.

I let out a short laugh. "Definitely. Totally on the straight and narrow now."

He laughed. It was a good laugh. Some people have an almost mean-sounding laugh. Some laugh like they don't mean it, like they're putting in actual effort to seem like they have a sense of humor. He didn't seem like that.

Then again, Connor had a great laugh, too. So apparently, it didn't mean all that much.

I felt a bit of my good mood fading. "Um. So I kind of want to surprise her with this, but there are a few things I can see right off that need to be fixed and I don't want her to have to deal with them."

He nodded. "Makes sense." He had a clipboard in his hand, and he clicked a pen. "I noticed two broken panes of glass in the front windows," he said, writing that down. I nodded.

"That. The front door sticks a little," I added, and he wrote that down, too. "Really, there's something that needs to be worked on in just about every room. And that's not even getting into the furnace or plumbing or anything like that, because I don't even know what to look for."

"I'll take a look at it while I'm here," he said, making a note of it.

"And charge me whether there's anything wrong or not?" I asked, semi-teasing.

He looked at me, a serious expression on his face. "I wouldn't do that," he said quietly.

"Why not? I just admitted that I wouldn't know either way."

"Because that's dishonest, and most of my referrals are word of mouth. I do a good job, so I get a lot of referrals. If I cheated people, that wouldn't happen." He met my eyes.

"And, you were just honest with me about not knowing. I'd be an absolute jerk to take advantage of that."

"Okay," I said. He was still studying me. "What?"

"You look kind of familiar," he said, and I tried not to react. My mask had fallen off during my fight with Maddoc, and it had been broadcast live on TV. For the most part, my face had been swollen and bloody, so I doubted many people would recognize me. My mother had, though.

I shrugged. "I'm just another blond chick. There are thousands of us, right?" I forced myself to smile.

"Maybe. Do you live around here?"

I shook my head.

"Hm. Well, let's see what else you want to add to the list, and then I'll get you a quote."

I took him through the house, room by room, pointing out all of the things I wanted fixed, from a broken light switch in the hallway to better fixtures in the bathroom. The wood floors throughout the house needed to be refinished, and the plaster was cracking in a few places on the ceiling and walls. There were a few more modern light fixtures that people had put in that didn't go with the house, and I pointed those out. When that was done, I led the way down to the basement and he took a look at the furnace and other mechanicals.

"This furnace is pretty new, actually," he said. "Water heater, too. The ductwork could use some insulating, though. These old houses are notorious for losing heat in the winter."

"Should we insulate anywhere else?" I asked, thinking of Mama's utility bills.

"I'll check out the attic. Probably wouldn't hurt to add some up there. And I'll check the windows and seal any that need it."

I nodded. "So… how much do you think this is going to cost? Ball park, I mean."

He looked over the list, and I studied him while pretending not to. He wasn't super tall, maybe six inches taller than me, I guess. Nicely built, but not as muscular as the guys I worked with. After a little while, he gave me a quote.

"It could change, but you asked for a ball park number. We'd go through an itemized thing if you decide to go forward, of course, and I'd spec out each item so you could sign off on only the ones you want done."

I nodded. I really wasn't worried about the money. I still had more than enough set aside, even after buying the place. Actually, I'd been expecting the number to be higher. "And how long do you think this will take?"

"Well." He looked around. "Less than a month, probably. Two to three weeks, if I hit it full time. Which, based on how much we're looking at, I wouldn't schedule any other jobs until I'm finished with this one, so I can give it my full attention."

"Do you do all the work, or do you have a crew that comes in to help you?"

"My brother works with me sometimes, when it's something I need more than just myself for. He'll probably be here to help out with the upstairs bath and maybe when I'm refinishing the floors, because that's just a lot faster with two guys. Is that okay?"

I nodded. "That sounds great. I think I'd like to go ahead."

He smiled. "Perfect. Let me write this up more officially, and we'll get a work order going." He went over to the kitchen counter, pulled a form out of his clipboard, and started writing. I wandered through the house a bit, rather than stand there staring at him like an idiot. My phone rang, and my stomach lurched. I pulled it out of my pocket and glanced at the number. Connor.

I looked at it for a moment, then answered.

"Hey. I'm back in town and I hadn't heard from you. How's everything?" he asked, and all I could think of was the photo of him, as Raider, standing over the dead body of a super hero. Less-than-pleasant comments about what he expected from me.

I gestured to Justin that I was going to step outside, and he nodded. I walked toward the front door then stepped out onto the porch before speaking.

"You lied to me," I said quietly.

"Oh, come on. I came clean. That was the whole point of that. To tell you so that we could move forward— "

"Not about that. You said you never…" I couldn't say the words out loud. "That British hero," I said, hoping he'd get what I was saying.

"I didn't say I never did that. I asked if it mattered. And you didn't answer." He paused as I fumed. "So you were researching me, Jolene?"

"What? Did you just expect me to let it go? To lap up more of your lies like a moron? I've done that too much already," I hissed.

"You're over-reacting."

My jaw dropped, and I couldn't even say anything for a few moments. "I don't think you can over-react about something like that," I finally said. "And besides that, there's the whole 'you blatantly lied to me' thing. Which really pisses me off, by the way."

"I did what I had to do then. Just like I'm doing now," he said in a flat tone.

"What else have you lied about?" I asked. "Is anything you've ever said to me the truth?"

"Oh, for fuck's sake," he muttered. "Of course."

"Which part?"

"I want you. I respect you and your powers. I am doing what I think is right— "

"Have you killed anyone lately?" I asked, so quietly I wondered if he even heard me.

"Don't worry about it," he said after a while, and my stomach sank.

"So you have."

"Don't fuckin' judge me, Jolene," he said harshly. "You're no innocent, either. Thief, liar, cheat. I came clean with you because I figured you'd understand. Didn't realize you were such a hypocrite."

"I've never killed anyone," I said, wishing he was in front of me so I could punch him. "That's a whole other level— "

"Oh, please," he snarled. "You spend too much time with assholes in spandex. Costumed heroes are a joke, and every single one of you thinks you're better than everyone else."

"I don't think I'm better than anyone."

"Bullshit. If you didn't, I wouldn't be getting a fuckin' lecture right now, when I was calling to see if you wanted to go out tonight."

"So...what? I'm supposed to feel guilty or something now? For confronting you about your bullshit?"

"I should have just screwed you that night and let it be. You would have happily done it, too," he said, and his voice was cold. It wasn't a tone I'd ever heard from him. I felt the last bit of hope that I was wrong about what a jerk he actually was vanish. It was like a balloon popping, deflating instantly.

"All that shit. All that 'you're so strong, Jolene,' 'smart girl,'" I said, mimicking him, repeating something he called me every once in a while. "The socks. All of it was bullshit."

"I meant some of it," he said coolly. "It didn't take much, did it? So close to getting what I wanted, and all I had to do was toss a few nice words and an ugly pair of socks I bought on clearance at Kmart in your direction. You are pathetic."

"Don't call me again," I said.

"I don't plan on it, sweetheart," he said, the word a snide twist on the way he had once said it. I hit the "end call" button and shoved the phone back in my pocket. I took a few deep breaths.

Well. I guess I dodged a bullet with that one. At least I found out what he was before it went any further. It hurt, actually. More than I'd expected it to. I didn't want to admit, even now, that I'd fallen for him.

And all of it was a lie. Every single bit of it.

I took another breath, then turned to go back into the house. Justin was still leaning on the kitchen counter, writing.

"Almost done. It was a long list," he said when he heard me walk in.

"Sure."

He glanced at me, pausing in his writing. "We can finish this up another time if you want. Or I can write this up and email it to you or something."

I shook my head. "It's fine. Just work bullshit… stuff," I said, irritated with myself. It's like I don't even know how to act around normal people sometimes.

He nodded, then went back to writing.

"I can get started tomorrow if you want."

"That would be great. I'll give you the extra key for the front door." I tried to keep myself calm, together.

It hurt. I've never even been close to being in love with someone before. I had no idea that this was what it felt like when something you had such high hopes for ends. I thought it would be easier, especially since I already knew he was lying to me. None of it had prepared me for hearing him talk to me the way he had, for the way the warmth I'd once heard in his tone had turned to icy derision.

Justin finished writing, and he handed me the forms. I mentally shook away the Connor issue to focus on what I was supposed to be doing. I looked over the list and the corresponding estimates, along with an initial quote for the work.

I gestured for the pen and signed and dated the bottom of the forms and handed them back to him. He gave me a copy of each one, then held his hand out and we shook on it.

"This place is going to look great. It's already a good house. A little bit of work, and you'll be proud to have your mom living here," he said. I let go of his hand.

"Thanks. I'm excited to see it. And thanks for agreeing to start on it so quickly."

I reached into my pocket and pulled the extra key off of the ring, handed it to Justin.

"My pleasure. I'll be here throughout the day, and if I need to finish stuff up, I'll probably be here some evenings, too."

"I don't want to take away from any other responsibilities you have," I said, feeling guilty that he expected to have to spend all of his time here.

He smiled. "My cat will get by, somehow," he said, and I gave him a small smile back.

"Okay. If you need to get in touch with me, you can always contact me at the number I gave you before."

"It should go pretty smoothly. I'll definitely call you before I do any painting, because I'd rather you pick the finishes in the house. Unless you want everything just to be painted white?"

I shook my head. "Mama can't stand white walls," I said.

"Okay. I'll call you then before the painting starts. And of course, any time you feel like checking in, do so."

"I don't want to get in your way," I said.

"You won't," he said, meeting my eyes briefly before looking away.

I gestured toward the door. "I have to get back to work, actually," I said.

"Sure." We walked out, and I noticed a large dark gray pickup truck parked near the curb. "It was a pleasure meeting you, Ms. Faraday," he said.

I smiled a little. "Jolene," I said. He nodded. "Have a good day."

"You too," he said. Then he gave me another small smile before walking toward his truck and climbing in. I watched him drive away, then started walking down the street. I locked up, then walked to the bus stop a few blocks away for the trip back to Command. It gave me plenty of time to think, but I wasn't so sure that was necessarily a good thing.

At least something good had happened today, I thought as I stared out the window. Mama's house was going to look great in just a few weeks. And I wouldn't waste any more thoughts or feelings on Connor, because he sure the hell wasn't wasting any on me.

I made it through the next few days alternately pissed off and depressed about how stupid I'd been over Connor, getting the silent treatment from my patrol partner, fielding dumbass questions from reporters and the "new media" assholes who were even worse, and just generally wanting to fall off the face of the planet for a while. On top of that were the dozen roses that Connor had sent to Command for me, in addition to the three voice mails he's left, telling me how sorry he was.

I was fed up with pretty much everything.

I finished up a patrol with Portia, since Dani had backed out on yet another shift and they needed someone to fill in, then made my way to the team lounge to see who was around. Mainly, I was hoping Jenson was around, because she'd been trying to get me to talk and I hadn't been in the mood and I kind of felt like a jerk for brushing her off all the time.

I walked into the team lounge to find Ryan, David, Amy, and Jenson in various states of slouch on the long couches there. Ryan was lying flat on his back, staring up at the ceiling and specifically not looking at me. Amy sat at the end of the couch, a book open in her hand, but she wasn't reading it. Jenson sat cross-legged on the other couch next to David, who had a tablet in his hand.

"Can't we turn this crap off?" Ryan was asking as I came in. "Why do you even follow that dipshit?"

"Because sometimes he's entertaining, and other times, he's kind of brilliant," David said.

"What dipshit?" I asked, sitting on David's other side so I could look at the tablet. On screen, there was a guy with a white mask over his face, sitting in an empty looking room. I listened for a moment. His voice was kind of distorted, the way they do on the news when they're trying to keep someone's identity a secret.

"This," David said, nodding toward the tablet. "Blogger, podcaster, livestreamer. The Detroit UnPowered guy?" he said, and I nodded, recognizing the name from hearing Portia complaining about him. "He records a new stream every couple days or so."

"What's with the mask?" I asked, and he shrugged.

"We can hardly point fingers about that, can we?" he asked.

I settled in next to him and watched. The guy sat at his desk, in front of his camera.

"It seems to me that Daystar isn't exactly what StrikeForce was expecting when she signed on. I've heard reports, and gotten tweets, emails, messages from all over the city that she's not only rude, but disrespectful as well."

"Oh, go fuck yourself," I muttered at the tablet, and my teammates laughed.

We listened as he went on, David still chuckling over the "rude" comment.

"And I was able to experience this first hand. And I wasn't the only one. I ended up at a crime scene where Daystar was one of the StrikeForce members who responded. I'll admit: she was fantastic in doing her job. She was amazing. Yes, I said it. I can respect what our city's heroes do when they do it well. As you all know, though, 'doing their jobs well' isn't exactly par for the course for StrikeForce."

"Should I say it again?" I muttered.

"He's not wrong," Jenson said quietly. "We all know that."

"But on this occasion," the streamer guy continued in his distorted voice, "this time, they did a great job. Particularly Daystar. We've all noticed that Daystar is not especially fond of the press. She doesn't like being looked at, and I wonder, sometimes, why that is. It's so out of character for super heroes, both in Detroit and in other cities. At any rate, one of the reporters, Bill Greenberg for the *News*, called out a question to Daystar. He said, pretty respectfully, actually, that it had been noted that her fighting style was different since that horrendous battle she had against Maddoc. Which is a fact. I've noticed it. Everyone who pays attention to this aspect of our lives had noticed it. So he bit the bullet and asked her about it. And she responded by holding up both middle fingers and taking off without another word."

"I wanted to do a hell of a lot more," I muttered. This was the last thing I needed, after the week I'd been having.

On screen, the streamer guy continued. "I guess I just think that we deserve better. This isn't the kind of behavior I think any of us need to see from the super powered beings who are supposed to be protecting us. It doesn't make any of us feel better to see this kind of... disdain for us."

"Why is he shitting on me?" I grumbled. "Caine does stuff like that all the time."

"You're a girl. You're supposed to be *nice*," Amy said with an eye roll.

"And don't forget the ever-popular 'likable,'" Jenson added.

"Such a bunch of bullshit," Amy said, and I gave her a surprised look. "Yes, Jolene. I curse sometimes. Don't look so shocked."

I laughed, and David looked over at me. "Is that really what it's like? All the time? Does everyone expect women to be nice?"

"It happens often enough," I said, thinking of my not-so-friendly phone conversation with Connor. "No matter what's said or done, if you stand up for yourself, if you're anything other than calm and cool about it, you're immediately an overly-emotional bitch. There is no in-between."

"Truth," Amy said.

"And that's a good example of it. That reporter was shouting out questions about kind of personal crap, bringing up some bad memories when I was supposed to be focusing on something else. So I was less-than-nice about it. And then you get assholes on the internet talking about how horrible you are," I said with a shrug. "It's nothing new."

David turned the stream off. "What an ass," he muttered.

"Keep watching him if you want. It doesn't hurt to know what they're saying about us. Is this guy popular or something?"

David nodded. "He was the first blogger to really focus on the super powered people here in Detroit. He has a huge following, including a bunch of national media outlets."

I thought that over for a while. "Well, just our luck that our local blogger is a dick, isn't it?" I asked. He laughed, and I patted his leg and stood up. "I'm going out for a while. I have my comm on if you need me."

"Want company?" Jenson asked.

"Sure."

Jenson followed me to the elevator, then we each went to our rooms to change into street clothes. She met me out in the corridor, and we took the elevator down to the lobby. "Where are we going?" she asked.

"I want to check on the work that's being done at the house I bought for Mama," I said. She gave me a look. "I'm paying for it with money I made before I started with StrikeForce," I said with a sigh. "Okay?"

"Okay."

"Do you still want to come?"

"Of course. You were so excited about this place, I'm kind of dying to see it."

"We'll walk to the bus stop down the block," I said. "I want to switch buses a few times before we get on the right one."

"Sounds good," she said.

"You don't think I'm being paranoid?" I asked, and she shook her head.

"We have enemies. It would be stupid not to do everything you could to cover your tracks and keep it all a secret. I'm doing the same thing," she reminded me. "I had to literally cry and beg to get my parents to do it, but they don't even live in the country anymore. I haven't seen them since this all started, because I'm too afraid some villain will figure it out. And you have more enemies than I do. More personal ones," she added after a moment.

I nodded. We walked, catching a bus on a route we didn't even want. We went through several bus changes, and then I felt okay about taking a bus to the Grosse Pointe border. We could walk to the house from there. We mostly rode in silence, but every once in a while we'd comment about a restaurant or something we were passing. I never really appreciated how freely we could talk to one another at Command versus out in public. Or it was kind of pathetic that our entire lives revolved around work, so that was all we had to talk about. Either way, we didn't say much during the ride.

We got off at the stop and started walking down Mack. It wasn't a long walk, and we could talk more freely now that we were alone.

"So, I meant to ask you... you seem kind of down the last few days. Is everything okay?" Jenson asked.

I shrugged.

"I mean, if you don't want to talk, it's fine. I won't be insulted. But if you do want to talk, I'm here," she said, shoving her hands in her pockets.

I took a breath. "It didn't work out with Killjoy," I said, looking straight ahead.

"Why not? What did he do?" she asked.

"He only wanted one thing, I guess. I thought it was more," I said, feeling stupid. "I called him out on some bullshit that he told me, and he didn't like that very much."

We walked in silence for a few moments. "This is why I don't date," she finally said. "I really thought you two maybe had something."

"That makes two of us," I admitted. "He told me some things I wasn't okay with, and he couldn't understand why. We got into a whole argument about it, and then it all just came out. I was stupid. It seemed too good to be true, too easy, because it was. He didn't know me. We only even talked a couple of times. And then there I am, daydreaming about forever like an idiot."

"You're human," she said. "And it's his loss."

"Yeah." We walked in silence for a while.

"My parents have been married for forty-seven years," she finally said, shaking her head. "I can't even imagine."

"You ever been married?" I asked her, and she shook her head.

"That is one mess I definitely don't need," she said with a smile. "I thought I would be, once, but then I got into a crazy situation — this was back when I was in the military — and I realized that I didn't want to put someone through that. I fully expect that I'm going to have a pretty short lifespan— "

"Why the hell would you say that?" I demanded.

"Please. I can self-replicate, but it's my only power. In a world full of people with super strength and toxic skin and healing factors, it's not exactly the kind of thing that anyone even looks at twice." She shrugged. "But I can do some good while I'm here, and who knows? Maybe I'll live to a ripe old age and get to ogle lifeguards on a tropical beach somewhere in my golden years."

I opened my mouth, then closed it. Then opened it again, trying to argue with her logic. Jenson laughed.

"That actually worked," she said, still smiling.

"What?"

"He doesn't seem very important now, does he?" she asked with a wink.

I stared at her, and she laughed again.

"I won't let anyone get to you," I said, still thinking it over.

She shook her head. "My point was, he's nothing. Yeah, you had some feelings for him, and they were maybe a mistake. But it's not life and death we're talking about here. It's one absolute asshole of a man."

"So, what? This is the girl equivalent of 'bros before hoes?'"

"Pretty much."

"You are nuts. I mean, you seem sane at first, but you're just as crazy as the rest of us," I said, and then I had to laugh.

"And you adore me, so there we go," she said.

By now, we'd reached the block with my mom's house on it, and I pointed it out to her. I made out the shape of the contractor's pick up truck in the driveway. "Looks like the carpenter is still here," I said.

We walked up to the house and I opened the front door. I could see Justin in the kitchen, bending over the kitchen counter, which was maybe half-covered with tiles that looked a lot better with the kitchen.

"Hey Justin. Just stopping by to see how it's going," I called.

"Great. I got a lot done on the second floor. Bath is done except for the paint, and all of the plaster repairs are done. I also sanded the floors up there for refinishing."

I raised my eyebrows at Jenson, and we headed up the stairs, Jenson looking around the entire time. "This is a great house," she said. "Reminds me of my grandma's house."

I nodded, and we looked in each room. I was amazed by how much he'd gotten done. This floor was ready for paint already, and I could see the cans of colors I'd picked out lining the hallway.

We headed back down. Justin was in the kitchen, apparently taking a break. He sat on a folding chair in the kitchen, steaming cup of black coffee in his hand.

"I can't believe how much you got done," I said.

"It went fast. Everything but the bathroom, but my brother came to help me with that."

Jenson nudged me, and I remembered that sometimes, people actually expect me to have manners. "Oh. Justin, this is my friend..." I turned to glance at her.

"Tina," she said, holding her hand out. Justin shook it. "Nice to meet you," she added.

Justin looked back at me. "So... how are you doing? Last time you were here, you seemed kind of stressed. Work stuff," he added.

"Much better. Work is still crazy, but I'm doing better," I said.

"What kind of work do you do again?" he asked.

"I'm a security guard," I said.

"Yeah, I bet that gets weird," he said. "Oh, before I forget, I double-checked the plumbing from the upper bath, and there was some corrosion and it looks like there was a small leak behind the wall on the first floor."

I groaned, and he held his hands up. "I fixed it. I was repairing the plaster in that room anyway. There was some staining on the wall, and I traced it back to that. I had to tear out some of the plaster, but I patched it and you shouldn't be able to see the difference once it's all painted."

"Thank you. Just add it to the invoice, then," I said.

I looked around. "It really is looking amazing. I feel like the house is in good hands. Can't wait to get Mama in here."

He ducked his head a bit, and I had the sense that he was pleased. He really was good looking. And handy. And polite. It was just too bad I was never, ever getting involved with anyone again. Ever.

"With any luck, it'll only take two weeks instead of the three I had planned. She'll be in here before the end of the month," he said, and I smiled.

Jenson's phone rang, and she glanced at it and quickly excused herself. I heard the front door open, then Justin and I were left in the kitchen.

"Can I ask you something?" I asked him, and he nodded. "How long have you been doing this?"

"Since I was a kid, really. My grandfather was a carpenter and he and my uncle worked together building custom homes out in the suburbs. Then my dad went into the business, and my brother and I just kind of ended up going along, too. Why?"

"You always hear horror stories about contractors who mess up more than they fix. I'm really grateful I don't have to deal with that. Makes my life easier. So thanks for having your crap together."

He laughed. "I try. Honestly, this job is the best one I've worked on in a while. There's a lot of original detail here to work with. Usually all the good stuff gets ripped out of these old houses."

I nodded. "That's part of what I liked about it. My mom pointed this house out, that she loved the way it looked from the outside, but I know she loves all of those old details, too, like the leaded glass windows and those built-ins in the living room."

He was watching me, and when he caught me looking, he glanced away.

"Do you like hockey?" he asked quietly, and I watched him.

"Yeah."

"Do you think you might want to go to a game sometime? I have season tickets," he said, meeting my eyes.

My stomach gave a funny little twist, but it was mixed with lingering disappointment.

"I mean... after this job is done," he added.

"I can't," I said. "Sorry."

He nodded. "Okay. Well, can't blame a guy for asking, right?"

I smiled. "It's been a while since anyone bothered," I told him, realizing that, actually, Connor had never asked me anything.

"I find that hard to believe," he said quietly, meeting my eyes again.

I shrugged. "Maybe I make a better first impression than I realized. Thanks for giving me an ego boost."

He chuckled. "Anytime. Let me know if you ever want your ego boosted again." He met my eyes for a brief moment, then we both glanced toward the door when Jenson came back in.

"That was my boss. I need to get back — can you give me a lift, Jolene?" she asked. I stood up.

"Sure." I glanced at Justin. "Thanks again. It really is looking great."

"Thank you. Nice meeting you," he said to Jenson, and she smiled. Jenson and I let ourselves out and started walking back down the block in the direction we'd come.

"Was that really work?"

"Yes. We have a Dr. Death sighting in Midtown. Figured you'd want in on it."

# CHAPTER NINE

Our "Dr. Death sighting" turned out, after five hours of searching, to be a bust. Ryan, Jenson, Ariana, and I all got back to Command shortly after midnight, more than a little frustrated and pissed off. I didn't doubt he'd been there. He was a Detroit super villain, after all. It was just that he was endlessly slipping through our fingers and now we knew that he'd been bargaining for samples of our blood for his experiments. It wasn't just me who had a personal hate on for him now, but no matter how badly we wanted to catch him, we still just kept hitting walls when it came to actually getting a hold of him.

I was still asleep when I heard the buzzer of my suite door going off. Which meant some asshole was wanting to talk to me at... I glanced at the clock.

Oh. It was after noon.

I got out of bed and ran a hand through my hair. I looked at the small monitor that allowed me to see the corridor, and I saw Ryan, Jenson, and David standing outside my door. I took a breath. This was probably going to be the kind of conversation that stressed me out.

I opened the door, and Jenson looked me over, a concerned expression on her face. "Were you still asleep?"

"Slept like crap," I answered. "Come on in." I waved them in and they walked past me. David stood near the window, and Jenson and Caine sat on the couch, and I took the chair and studied them. Jenson seemed the same, but David seemed kind of stressed and Ryan kind of looked like he wanted to destroy something, but maybe not me this time. "Okay. Spit it out. What's wrong?"

"That livestream guy? The Detroit Unpowered guy?" David said, and I rolled my eyes.

"Yeah, what about him? Did I disrespect somebody again?"

He looked grim, and exchanged a glance with Jenson.

"What? What is it?"

Jenson took a breath. "On last night's show, he put forth a theory he has about you."

"Okay. And? There are lots of theories about me."

"He believes you're the suburban burglar," she said. "He posted videos of you tearing down that motel in your burglar days, and then now. Pointed out similarities in how you move, in the angle you use when you take off flying, stuff like that. Judged your height and size…"

"It'll blow over," I said. I kind of felt like throwing up. I'd finally started to think that maybe everyone had forgotten about my burgling days.

"I don't think it will," David said. "Lots of people are backing his theory. It's all over on social media. Even the morning news on most of the local channels reported on it today."

"Shit," I groaned.

"They're calling for you to face the charges. Make a statement. They also want Alpha to come forward with what he knows about you."

I released a low, bitter laugh. "Well, that's just great."

"Portia is planning to do a press conference," Jenson said.

"To say what?"

"What do you think? That it's a ridiculous theory and she's disgusted by these unfounded attacks on a hero who has protected this city time and time again."

"We all know that's bullshit though," I said.

"Only the burglar part," Ryan said. "The rest is the goddamn truth."

"And nobody knows but us, and none of us are going to rat you out," Jenson said. "I say, let Portia do it. It'll all blow over. I mean, I don't doubt that he'll keep talking about it, because he is persistent if nothing else. But the rest of the public will forget about it eventually."

My mind was fixated on something she'd said. *None of us would rat you out.* But there were other people out there who knew who I was. What I was.

"You wouldn't rat me out," I said softly.

"Of course not," David said, and Jenson nodded.

"Killjoy knows," I said, meeting Jenson's eyes.

"Shit."

"Yeah."

"Wait. You and Killjoy are, like, together. Right?" David asked me, and I shook my head.

"And, he's not okay with that, exactly?" he asked with a pained look. I shook my head again.

"Shit," he muttered, repeating Jenson's response. We sat in morose silence for a little while, then David sat up again. "Just because he's not happy with you, that doesn't mean he'd rat you out. I mean, whatever happened between you, he's one of us. Kind of," he said, furrowing his brow. "I don't think he'd do that."

I kept to myself what Killjoy was. What he had been. What he maybe still was. I didn't want to have to admit exactly how stupid I'd been. How blind.

"And whether he does or not," Jenson said," I think we still move forward with Portia's presser regardless. And sooner rather than later. She's ready to do it today."

"Do you expect me to talk?"

Jenson and David exchanged a look, and Jenson finally spoke up. "It might be better if you didn't. You aren't exactly a patient, laid-back person," she said. "Unless you want to," she added quickly.

"No, I don't want to," I said, slumping back in my chair. "I'll lay low for a little while. I don't feel like answering stupid questions from asshole reporters right now."

Jenson stood up. "Okay. I'll tell Portia to do it. Hang in there, okay?"

I nodded. "Thanks."

Ryan stayed where he was, and Jenson and David left my suite to go talk to Portia.

He was silent for a few seconds, then he leaned forward and rested his elbows on his knees. "So… what did Killjoy do? Am I going to have to hunt him down and break his face? I mean, I might need you to help me, but…"

I smiled in spite of myself. At this point, I was just relieved to have him talking to me again. "I don't think any of us could break Killjoy's face."

"We could break it. But it would heal again and we'd have to break it again," he said, and I laughed. "What'd he do to you, Jolene?"

I shook my head. "We got into an argument. And I realized he wasn't who I thought he was. He didn't feel the way I thought he did. And I was too blinded by a bunch of muscles and a Scottish accent to see it."

Ryan kept his steady gaze on me. "Is he going to be a problem?"

I shrugged. "I hope not. I have no idea. He's pretty pissed at me and he doesn't strike me as the forgiving type. Mostly, I figure we'll just stay out of one another's way."

He sighed. "I'm sorry. He's an idiot."

I shook my head. "Let's talk about something else."

"Such as?"

"Such as, I really am sorry about before. It's nice to have you talking to me again."

"I just needed some time. I wasn't trying to give you the silent treatment. Just didn't know what to say. It bothered me more than I thought it would, that you knew shit and didn't tell me. I thought we had a certain level of trust. We need that, working together the way we do. I was kind of surprised, I guess, on top of being pissed."

"And I hope you believe me when I say that I wasn't specifically trying to hide things from you. I was thoughtless, but I wasn't trying to be sneaky."

A small smile lifted the corner of his mouth. "No, I get that. Though you have to admit that when you do sneaky, you're pretty good at it."

"Former burglar," I said with a shrug, which brought us back to the Detroit Unpowered guy. "It would be kind of great if we could get this streamer guy to obsess on someone else."

"Agreed. Maybe we'll send him some anonymous tips about Death and Daemon and those assholes. You know, people who are actually worth criticizing."

I nodded. We sat in silence for a few moments. "For the record, it's good to be talking to you again, too," he finally said.

"Thanks. I'll try to be better about the whole trust thing. It isn't something I've had to deal with very much. I'm really good at keeping things to myself, though."

He nodded.

"Like your name," I said quietly. I looked up to see him watching me. "Do you regret telling me?"

"No. I don't regret it at all," he answered, meeting my eyes.

"And I promise I won't make you regret it. Portia said no one knows your name. Including her," I added.

"Nobody does."

"But I do."

He took a breath. "I figure you've had enough secrets and lies by now from the people you're supposed to be working with. And so have I. I think we both deserve better. Don't you?"

I nodded.

He met my eyes for a moment, then he stood up and let himself out of my suite. I watched as he closed the door behind himself, relieved that he wasn't pissed at me anymore.

And then it hit me that my mother had probably heard Detroit UnPowered's theory already via the news as well.

"Shit."

I took a bus to Mama's neighborhood and walked the rest of the way to the entrance of the trailer park, then scuffled down Perdition Lane toward our little yellow and white trailer. Mama's car was, as expected, sitting there in the driveway. She was always off on Fridays.

I skipped up the steps and knocked. Mama answered the door, pushing it open silently. She closed it, then looked up at me.

"Is it true, Jolene?"

"What do you think?" I asked, which I knew was a coward's way to answer.

"I don't know what to think right now." She shook her head and walked toward the tiny galley kitchen. "I did wonder sometimes where you went in the evenings, but I figured you maybe had a boyfriend, or girlfriend, or something that you were keeping to yourself until you were ready to tell me. And then the superhero thing came out and I figured, well, that had to be it!" She paused, leaning against the kitchen counter. "Just tell me, Jolene. Is it true?"

I answered my mother the same way I would have answered anyone else. Which makes me an absolute piece of shit.

"No, Mama. Of course it's not true. That Detroit UnPowered guy is delusional. And Portia's having a press conference later today to tell everyone so."

"Why aren't you going to be at the press conference?"

I smiled. "Come on. You know me better than anyone. Do I handle that kind of thing well? Talking in public, let alone being accused of something in such a public way? It's much better to have Portia handle it, and it'll all blow over. I just heard a little while ago, actually, and I figured you'd heard, too."

She sighed, then smiled. "I knew he was full of it. You've always been a good girl."

I forced myself to smile back. I was definitely, absolutely going to hell and I was a terrible person. I'd keep trying to make myself into the person my mother believes I am, but it's not smooth going. Maybe someday, I'll get there.

"Do you want me to make lunch? Can you stay?" she asked, and I thought about turning it down, but in the end, I didn't want to. After all of the stuff with Connor, then this mess, I wouldn't have minded going back to being a little kid again, having Mama taking care of me.

"Sure." She made grilled cheese sandwiches and we at down at the little dinette table and ate and talked. It took everything in me not to spill the beans about the house, but I figured maybe it wasn't the best time, because she'd immediately wonder now where I got the money. Another couple of weeks, and the house would be ready and this stupid mess will have all been a memory.

We watched Portia's press conference together, where she calmly and coolly refuted the theory that I was ever a burglar, going over my many brave deeds, the people I've saved, and reminding everyone that I had paid, nearly dying, trying to make Mayhem pay for the lives they'd destroyed a few weeks back.

"She nearly gave her life. She nearly lost it all, and we're standing here today questioning whether she's a good person or not. Think about that. And then think about the fact that maybe we should stop considering anonymous streamers and bloggers to be acceptable news sources. Thank you."

"I like her," Mama said after it ended.

"Me too. She's a good one."

"I'm surprised it wasn't Alpha out there. He always seemed to love giving speeches."

I shrugged. "He's taking a more behind-the-scenes approach to leadership," I said. It wasn't technically a lie. He was way, way behind the scenes. "And Portia's just so good at this," I said, gesturing toward the screen.

"She really is," Mama agreed.

I stayed for a little while longer, then I hugged her goodbye and made my way back to Command. I snagged a few slices of pizza from the dining hall and took them up to my suite. I settled down on my couch with the pizza and my laptop and started searching, seeing what I could find out about the masked streamer.

After about an hour, I was starting to get frustrated. Not even a hint of who he was when he wasn't wearing the mask. A knock at my door shook me out of my reverie, and I got up and let Jenson in. She glanced at my laptop, which was playing an older stream of his, and raised her eyebrows.

"Trying to figure out who he is. Where he is," I said, flopping down on the couch. She sat next to me. "I wonder if David could track it somehow."

"Normally, he could. He's tried already," she said, and I looked at her in surprise. "You're not the only one annoyed right now, you know. We'd rather not have our friends messed with."

"Thanks."

She waved it off. "He tried. And this guy's not stupid. Covers his tracks, has his sites set up as mirrors so you can't really tell what the originating source is. All David's hit has been dead ends."

We sat and watched for a couple of minutes. "Seriously, what the hell does a blogger need a secret identity for anyway?" I asked in irritation. I glanced over at Jenson to see her smirking.

"What?"

"Maybe because sometimes he ends up with pissed off super-powered people cyberstalking him."

I glared at her, and she laughed.

"Just a theory," she said, and I shook my head.

"How's the training coming? I meant to ask you. Caine said you did really well when he trained with you."

I shrugged. "Well enough, I guess. I really do need to hit the training room with him more. It seems like there's always something going on, and now I'm trying to make sure Mama's house gets done." I shook my head. "Did you guys uncover anymore files? Anything beyond what you guys showed me before?"

Jenson shook her head. "There were three more files he was able to crack, but they were all personal emails between Alpha and Crystal."

"Personal?"

"As in, details about what they wanted to do to each other. Lots and lots of detail," she said with a grimace.

"Ew."

"Yes. I wish brain bleach was a thing and I kind of hate David for showing them to me."

I laughed. "So we're still going with the theory that this was some kind of injection to give people powers?"

Jenson nodded.

"And that this was Dr. Death negotiating with Alpha?"

She nodded again.

"Have we asked Alpha and his people about that?"

"Of course. None of them will say a word. Either way, Portia feels that we have enough evidence to turn them over to international custody. And I'm looking forward to it. The sooner we get them out of here, the better."

"And then we lose Alpha's money."

"We all knew that was happening anyway. And that's why you've been socking money away, right?"

I nodded.

"I still think it was wrong, but it made some sense. He likely won't even miss it."

137

"Wishing you'd let me siphon a little more?" I asked with a smirk, and she rolled her eyes. We sat in silence for a few moments. "It's going to be a bit of a shake up when it all comes out. This guy's gonna have a field day," I said, gesturing toward my laptop, where the streamer was talking about the dangers of masked heroes again.

"Well. We knew that, too. We'll get through it. And we still have a little time. The international tribunal moves about as quickly as ents."

"You are such a nerd," I said. "I bet you even speak elvish."

She stood up, muttering "*Auta miqula orqu.*"

"I knew it! What did you say?"

She just rolled her eyes and let herself out, chuckling softly as she left.

# CHAPTER TEN

I took the bus to Grosse Pointe again. One thing I was already liking about Mama's house was that checking on it gave me a good excuse to get out of Command once in a while. And the bus rides gave me time to think.

I was sitting on the bus, looking out the window and letting my mind wander, when my phone rang, and my stomach flipped a little when I realized which ring it was.

I looked at the phone, then answered it. "Yes?" I asked.

"Hey," Connor said. I hated how just that one syllable made me respond, how it made my chest hurt and my stomach twist. After a couple of moments, he spoke again. "How have you been?"

"I've been better," I said.

"Yeah. I saw that shit on the news. Portia did a good job addressing it."

"It wasn't just that."

I heard him take a breath. "I know. I'm sorry, sweetheart. The shit I said... I don't even know why I said it. I didn't mean any of it. I'm crazy about you and I alway have been. You have to know that. I said that shit because I was upset, and I never should have said it."

I swallowed, caught between emotions. I wanted so badly to believe him. But my heart told me otherwise. There'd been no deceit in the angry words he'd thrown at me, in the way he'd insulted and belittled me. I watched it happen too many times with Mama and my dad. He'd be an asshole, and the next day, it would be all sweetness and compliments, and then things would go back to normal until he snapped again. I remember Mama telling me once, when I was a teenager, to turn and run the second a man tried to treat me like shit, because he'd do it again.

"No. I think you meant every word you said."

"Jolene, I want you, sweetheart. I miss you. You have to know that."

"I think it's better if you don't call me anymore. I said it last time, and I did actually mean it."

"You didn't. You were pissed, and you had every reason to be. Just... let's go out to dinner tonight and try to talk about this, huh? We can work this out. We're worth fighting for."

I bit my lip. I'd already made mistakes with him. I wasn't going to make any more.

"We're done, Connor. I really don't want to hear from you again."

He was quiet for a few beats, then he sighed. "Fine. Suit yourself." And then he hung up, and I sat there wishing it could have been different. That we would have been okay and he'd never lied to me. That he was all of the things I'd thought he was. But he wasn't, and I couldn't try to fool myself into thinking he was.

I stuffed my phone back into my pocket and went back to staring out the window. By the time the bus pulled up to my stop, I felt a little lighter, a little better than I had. I felt stronger. I'd get through this, and I would be okay.

I walked up to the house, noting that the living room and kitchen lights were on. Justin's truck was pulled up into the driveway. As I mounted the front steps, I saw Justin cross in front of the windows. When I opened the front door, he peered around the wall between the living room and dining room.

"Hey," he said, stopping. "I was wondering if I'd see you today."

"Really?"

"Yeah. You stop in every three days. I was hoping this would be another lucky day," he said with a smile, and I shook my head.

"Smooth, Justin," I said, and he laughed.

"I meant it, too," he said, and I met his dark eyes for a moment before looking away. "I finished painting the upstairs, so that floor is completely done now if you want to take a look at it," he said after a moment.

"You move fast," I said, heading toward the stairs.

"Not as fast as I'd like, sometimes," he answered, and I had the feeling that maybe he wasn't just talking about the house. I felt a blush heat my cheeks as I walked up the stairs in front of him.

The first thing I noticed was the the dark wood floors absolutely gleamed. The hallway was painted a clean cream color with white trim. I peeked into the bathroom to find a soft pink, which my mother would love. The front bedroom and second bedroom were a soft, buttery yellow, and the other small bedroom on the floor was a soothing sage green.

"This looks so good," I said quietly. "I figure, with those built-ins, she can have a little library in here. It's a cozy room."

He nodded. "It would be perfect for that."

"You've done an amazing job already."

He didn't answer, and I glanced up to see him looking down at me. I felt a pang of regret again. Once upon a time, I would have been brave enough to take a chance on the mouth-watering carpenter with the deep, warm voice. His eyes alone were enough to make me want to take a leap of faith, but I just didn't have it in me. I looked away, digging a check out of my pocket.

"Here. For the work you've done already. I wanted to keep up with the invoicing," I explained.

"Thanks. This will make billing easier once it's finished."

I nodded.

We walked back downstairs and the doorbell rang. Justin went to the front door and said a few words to whoever was on the porch. When he came back to the living room, he was holding a large pizza box.

"Well. I'm planning to stay late and finish up that mess of plumbing in that first floor powder room. Do you feel like eating with me?"

"I shouldn't."

"You'd be saving me. I definitely shouldn't eat the whole thing," he cajoled.

"I think you'd be fine, somehow."

"Pizza's dangerous. Seriously, it'll go straight to my ass and then I'll have self esteem issues…"

I laughed. "Right. Because you so obviously have that problem."

"Come on. Help me, Jolene," he said with a smile. He opened the pizza box, wiggled it a little, trying to entice me to take a piece.

"Fine," I said with a sigh. I grabbed a slice and he grinned. He sat down on the living room floor and set the pizza box down, and I sat beside him. We ate in silence for a few minutes.

"Security guard, huh?" he asked.

"It's a temporary thing. I want to do community outreach stuff eventually," I said, remembering the things I'd wanted when I'd started college. The ideas I'd had about what I'd do if I ever had enough power and money. I shrugged. "For now, it pays the bills, you know?"

"Based on how much you probably paid for this house, plus what you're paying me, it more than pays the bills."

"I've been socking money away. I don't really spend much otherwise. I knew I wanted to do this eventually."

Justin nodded. "You should find a house like this for yourself."

"I don't know if I'm the house type. I'm not home much."

"You'd be surprised. I thought the same thing, and then I bought my first house, fixed it up. The plan was to flip it, sell it at a profit, but I couldn't do it. It's nice feeling like there's a place that's just yours, you know?"

I nodded. "That's what I want for Mama. Maybe someday, I'll want it for myself." I took another bite of pizza. "So where's your house?"

"Indian Village."

"Expensive area," I commented.

"My house was the blight in the neighborhood. I got it for a steal because it was about to be torn down. It took me almost a year to get it livable."

"You must be persistent," I said.

"You have no idea."

I glanced up to see him watching me again.

"And a complete professional," I reminded him.

He looked away. "Right."

I shifted a little. This was stupid. I shouldn't be sitting here. This guy and I had nothing in common, even if you didn't count the whole super powered thing. And the fact that I wasn't looking for anything like what I had a feeling would happen between us if I just let go a little bit.

"It's not you, you know," I blurted. His dark eyes met mine, and I went on before I lost my nerve. "I just ended what I thought was maybe something... something more than it actually was. I don't trust my judgment right now and I don't know when I will. Just... it's not you," I repeated.

He sat there for a moment, silently studying me. "Okay," he finally said. "Thanks for telling me that. I know what that's like. Went through it a few years ago, and I'm just glad I figured it out before it was too late. Before there was a wedding or kids or anything like that."

"Right. But I don't think this is exactly the same."

"Maybe not," he said with a shrug. "All I know is that when it was over, I felt like an idiot. Like I'd been the butt of her private joke the entire time we'd been together. And I figured I had lousy taste in women."

"Maybe you still do," I said, dropping my pizza crust back into the box. I stood up, and so did he.

"Kinda doubt it." He finally looked away from me. "You know, it doesn't have to be the type of thing that leads to us getting married. We can just have fun."

"So all you want is a booty call type of thing?" I asked.

He met my eye again. "No. If I wanted that, I would have said so. I meant, we can hang out. Go places. Yeah, maybe see if I can make you moan, because I'd be lying if I didn't admit that I would be up for the challenge."

"No pun intended, huh?" I asked with a smirk, even though I could feel my face burning.

"Pun very much intended, actually," he said in a low voice. I looked away.

"Well. Like I said, I'm not looking for anything at all like that right now. My life is too crazy and I'm pretty sure it would just end badly. And who knows? Maybe I'd want to hire you again but if we hated one another, that would be awkward, so.... yeah," I said with a shrug.

"Very practical," he said, and I caught a glint of humor in his dark eyes.

"And I can promise you that that is something no one has ever accused me of being before," I said. I stood up, and so did he.

I looked down at his hands, which were strong, calloused, and large. I fought back a little shiver. "Um. I should probably go."

"Worried you might do something stupid?" he asked.

I started stepping away. "Maybe."

"Jolene."

"Yeah?"

"I just thought I should tell you that you have a gorgeous ass. It was a pleasure following you up the stairs."

"I— "

"And I enjoy seeing you blush like that."

"This is very unprofessional," I said backing away another step.

He stepped forward. "Then fire me."

And the next thing I knew, his lips were on mine, his hand buried into my hair, holding my head at the angle he wanted me. This wasn't a timid kiss. It was hot, hungry, and I had the sense that he was holding back, that what he really wanted to do was kiss me senseless. He gave my hair a light pull, moving my head to the side a little, and I heard a tiny moan escape my throat.

I kissed him back. Damn it, I am a stupid bitch, but I kissed him back and I liked it. When Connor had kissed me, it had been fleeting, the barest meeting of lips, like he was doing the bare minimum that one could call "kissing." But this… this was something else, the way Justin's lips crushed mine, the way his tongue invaded my mouth and his teeth nipped and pulled at my lower lip. I pressed my hands to his chest, initially to push him away, and instead I found myself clinging to him, gathering big handfuls of his t-shirt in my fists.

I wanted to feel bad about this, to have the sense to push him away. Whether it was my battered ego or just being pissed at Connor, I wanted this for myself, in the moment. I wanted to feel good, and kissing Justin… it felt beyond good, and I kissed him in a way I don't think I'd ever kissed anyone before.

When he finally drew back, it felt like my entire body was about to combust. I have never, ever been kissed the way he kissed me, as if he was in total control, confident, taking what he wanted from me while making damn sure that I got plenty in return. I stood still as a statue, my lips swollen from his attention, my heart racing, my hands trembling, and I stared at him.

He looked perfectly calm and collected, as if the entire earth hadn't just shifted beneath our feet.

"Still think we shouldn't give this a shot?" he asked in a rough voice.

"Do you plan on trying to convince me some more?" I asked, and he let out a low laugh that sent shivers up my spine.

"Don't tempt me," he said mildly. I didn't answer and after a moment, he took a breath. "Just, let's be clear that I'm not him, whoever was before me that has you convinced you're not going to manage a good relationship."

"Yeah, I kinda got that. And I'm still not ready for this."

He nodded and took a step away. "Okay. Did you want me to apologize for kissing you?"

I shook my head.

"Good. Because it would be a lie. I should get back to work."

"Okay. Thanks for the pizza."

"Thanks for the kiss," he said, meeting my eyes again. Then he turned and headed toward the back of the house. "Talk to you later."

I went out the front door and down the front walk, then turned and looked at the house from the sidewalk. After a moment, I did what I was pretty sure I'd always do, what I'd always been doing in one way or another: I walked away. I know what my limits are. What I can handle at any given time. And the man in that house wasn't something I could handle now. I had a mother to move. A super powered injection creator to find. An ex who was an even bigger jerk than I am, and a billionaire held captive in StrikeForce's basement. My best friend had caught me stealing money, my partner was just getting over being majorly pissed with me, and some dickhead blogger was way too observant for anybody's good.

I kind of had a full plate.

Still, it had been nice to be reminded that Connor wasn't the end for me. He would just be a constant reminder to watch myself, to look before I leap. And to not get involved with lying assholes.

# CHAPTER ELEVEN

I got back to Command and made my way up to my room, glad that I managed not to bump into anyone. For the moment, I just wanted to be alone.

Once I was back in my room, I stripped and stepped into the shower. The cool water didn't do much to soothe the way my body was still overreacting to that damn kiss. As I washed and shampooed, I kept forcing my mind away from Justin's hands, to imagining what it would have been like to have his hands on my body.

"So stupid," I muttered to myself with a grin as I rinsed off. I tore my mind away from him again, reminding myself that I promised Mama I'd call her tonight, because she'd had a dialysis appointment and I wanted to check on her. I always offered to go with her, and she always turned me down. She preferred to go alone. I guess I understood. She didn't want me to see her when she felt weak or tired. Mama was always one to keep burdens to herself, even if I wished she'd let me help her more.

Well, she was getting a nice new house in a pretty neighborhood whether she wanted it or not. And one of these days, I'd even convince her to retire.

I smiled to myself as I dried off and slipped into my ratty old flannel pajama pants and a U of D t-shirt. I called

Mama, and she filled me in on her day. I settled into bed and chatted with her for a while. She filled me in on her day at work, about a couple of patients she'd dealt with, and I talked about a guy we'd brought into Command earlier that day who had x-ray vision. He'd been reported for being pervy at a local mall once women started realizing what he was up to. Mama laughed, and then tried to stop.

"I shouldn't laugh at that, really. But what teenage boy didn't dream of power like that?" she asked with a laugh.

"Hell. I can imagine that there are plenty of grown men and women who'd appreciate it," I said, and she laughed again. "Oh, Mama — You're off on the fifteenth, right?" I asked, remembering the date Justin expected to be finished with the house. I wanted to show it to her as soon as possible, and it was only a few days away now.

"I am, unless I get called in. Why?"

"I have a little surprise for you and it's supposed to be ready then."

"Surprise? What surprise?" she asked.

"If I told you, it wouldn't be a surprise now, would it?" I teased.

"Jolene Marie Faraday," she scolded, and I laughed. "A hint?"

"Nope."

"Evil child," she said with a laugh.

"But you love me."

"More than anything."

I smiled. "I should let you go. I just wanted to check in with you. I love you, Mama," I said.

"Love you more, Ladybug. Good night," she said, and I listened as the call disconnected. I nodded to myself as I set my phone down. She was going to freak out when she saw the house.

I snuggled down into bed, pulling my blanket up over my nose. I had just closed my eyes when my phone rang.

I groaned.

I did not feel like fighting any super-powered assholes. I wanted to go to sleep and not think.

I picked the phone up, glancing at the screen, which said "unknown." I considered not answering. It was probably a telemarketer or some shit like that. Or a reporter finally managed to track down my personal phone number.

It could actually be important though, I thought, and I answered.

"Is this Daystar?" a man's voice said on the other end of the phone. Vaguely familiar.

"Yes. Who is this?"

"How are your ribs?"

There was silence for a few moments, when it clicked. Dr. Death. That slight accent, the smooth tone.

"How did you get this number?"

"Oh, a little Virus bird told me." Damian. Fuck.

"So what do you want?"

"I think you can guess what I want. I want my associates released from your custody. And I want a sample of your blood for my little pet project."

I laughed at him.

"I assure you I am not joking. You have until four o'clock tomorrow afternoon to return my associates, and one of them will have a vial of your blood."

"Yeah? And if I don't?"

"You won't be happy with what happens next. Four o'clock, Daystar. Not a moment longer." And with that, the call came to an end.

I sprang out of bed and carried my phone down to David's lab. He was, as always, hunched over his keyboard. Jenson sat in a chair beside him, looking at her tablet.

"Hey," I said, and they both looked up.

"What's up?" Jenson asked, studying my face. "Something happened."

"Dr. Death just called me at this number. Said he got the number from Damian."

"What did he want?" David asked, taking my phone.

I relayed his demands to them, and they both said that he must be crazy. Which was obvious. "Can you trace it or anything?" I asked David.

He was already poking around in the settings of my phone. "You really should start using your official phone. We have all kinds of tracking and other stuff set up on those. Yours is pretty locked down and the tracker we install on the official phones isn't here." I didn't bother mentioning that I knew the official phones had all that shit on them, which was why I didn't use them. I figured that calling my fence from an official StrikeForce phone might just be the kind of thing that would piss her off.

"So you can't?" I asked him, and he shook his head.

"What do you think he meant? About what will happen?" I asked.

David shrugged. "Knowing Dr. Death, he'll try to turn more innocent people into super powered freaks. We'll increase patrols throughout the city tomorrow, especially after four, so we'll be ready. I mean… you're not considering trying to meet his demands, are you?"

"Oh, hell no. I mean, does he seriously think I'd do either of the things he wanted?"

Jenson had been quiet for the entire conversation, and I looked at her. "What's wrong?" I asked. "Other than the obvious, I mean."

She shook her head. "That demand. Coming to you directly with it. He could have brought it to Portia as our team leader. He could have called it in to any of us. And it's so ridiculous… he has to know you'd never comply with it."

I shrugged. "He's a super villain. I think we can assume he's nuts."

She furrowed her brow and shook her head again. "It just kind of reeks of desperation. I wonder if there's something going on. Something we're not seeing. I mean, why the rush now?"

"Probably just got tired of waiting," David said. "You know how these villain assholes are. They make demands. I'm pretty sure it's part of the villain handbook or something, right after 'how to deliver a villainous monologue.'"

"Yeah. He usually keeps a pretty low profile, though. Contacting us directly isn't really his style," Jenson said.

I shook my head. "Well. I'll go fill Portia in," I said. "I really wish we would have gotten this asshole last time."

"Next time," David reassured me. "We'll get him next time. Which will probably be tomorrow, I guess."

"Great. Let's just hope he doesn't manage to harm too many people before we manage it."

"Stop, Jolene," Jenson said.

"What?"

"Blaming yourself for not getting him before," she said. "That's on us, not you. And David's right. We'll get him this time, lock him up, and throw away the key."

I nodded, then waved at the two of them and left, heading up to Portia's office on the top floor. By the time I'd filled her in with all of the details and gotten her agreement that we should increase patrols, everyone on duty, it was into the wee hours of the morning and I felt dead on my feet.

# CHAPTER TWELVE

At our morning meeting, Portia filled the entire team in on Dr. Death's phone call and his demands, as well as his threat. She went over the plan, to have everyone on the street around four to ensure that if he did pull anything like what he'd pulled before in Midtown, we'd be able to act on it quickly. The team was quiet. I knew each of us was thinking of the last time. Of almost three dozen still, lifeless bodies on the street near the art museum. Of the beating we'd taken afterward. Caine spoke up first.

"Somebody should be with Jolene all day."

"I think I'm safe," I said.

He shook his head. "This doesn't strike anyone else as weirdly personal? Why go to Jolene with this?"

"Exactly what I said," Jenson said.

"Because it's her blood he wants for his stupid little injection project. We know that already from the files David cracked," Portia said.

"For that, whatever. But why go to her about the prisoners? She's not in charge here. She has no authority to set anyone free."

"Well, she's done it before," Chance said. We all looked at her, surprised. She rarely talks, and it's pretty easy to forget that she's even there. "I mean... when Alpha was holding Amy and the others," she added, then looked down and away.

"Yeah, but he doesn't know that," Caine said.

"Unless one of the people who decided to leave went to Dr. Death," David said.

"That electro bitch. I knew we should have kept here here," Monica said. "She hated you," she told me.

"Thanks, Monica."

She flipped me the bird, grinning. I shook my head and continued listening to Caine and Portia argue about how it should all be handled.

"I think Portia's instructions are best," I said. "Sticking me with someone all day long will just be an extra burden. Plus, I'll be on patrol with Jenson and David after four, right, for the increased patrols? And I'm around here all day monitoring shit. I'm the least of our worries right now."

"Agreed," Portia said, and that closed the matter. We split, each of us going to deal with our assigned tasks.

I spent the day monitoring traffic cameras, social media feeds, anything that would alert us to something weird happening. We never bothered with traditional media for that kind of thing. They were always about a day behind what people managed to catch with their phones. In general, it seemed quiet.

I tried not to think about what might happen. We'd spent a good part of the day trying, again, to get Death's buddies in the prison wing to tell us where he was. Or, I should say, Portia and Amy tried. I urged them to let me in to talk to them, but neither of them trusted me once things got frustrating. And they always got frustrating with Death's crew.

As the clock inched closer to four o'clock, I started getting more and more tense. My stomach was a tight knot of stress.

At ten to four, Jenson and David came into the command meeting room. "Ready to patrol, Jolene?" Jenson asked.

I shook my head. "Go ahead, I'll meet up with you. I want to keep an eye on things for a couple more minutes. Maybe it was a bluff."

"Okay. We've got Wayne State and Midtown," David said, and I nodded and turned back to the screen.

The alarm on my phone beeped at four o'clock. I clicked it off and kept my eyes glued to the monitors. Seconds later, my phone rang. Not the regular voice phone, though. The video chat app. Unknown source.

I took a deep breath and hit the "accept call" button. Death appeared on the screen. He seemed to be inside. I couldn't tell where.

"I did warn you, Daystar," he said calmly. "All you had to do was comply. This is your fault. This is what your foolish bravado earns you."

"What?"

"Tell me. Do you know this woman?" Death asked, and then he pulled the phone back so I could see more of the background. It looked like a hospital. Clean white floors. And there, at the reception desk, wearing her usual pink scrubs, was Mama.

"Don't even think about it," I said, jumping up.

"Oh, my dear. I was having coffee and a chat with your darling mother at four o'clock. It appears... something awful made it into her coffee."

At that moment, my mother fell over, and I could see bloody foam at her mouth. I screamed, and then I ran up the flight of stairs to the flight deck and took off.

"I did warn you," Death said again, and then the call ended.

I flew faster. She worked at Detroit Receiving, which wasn't too far from us. I don't think I've ever flown so fast in my life. If she had to get poisoned, a hospital was the place for it to happen. They'd pump her stomach and she'd be fine.

That's what I told myself as I flew, as I landed outside the hospital.

As I barely noted the crowd of doctors and other hospital staff in the lobby, the crush of bodies, the sirens. In the middle of it all, Mama lay on the floor, that awful pinkish-red foam covering her chin. I shoved someone aside and knelt next to her. A doctor was kneeling over her on the other side.

"Can you pump her stomach? You can save her, right?" I asked him. He looked at me in surprise. He was a young doctor, A glance at his badge showed the name Dr. Gupta, M.D., OB.

"She is gone," he said softly.

"That's not possible. This just happened. She ingested something," I said. I knew my voice was getting louder, more desperate.

"She's— "

"Try something!" I shouted, and he stared at me.

He told one of the nurses to bring him some things. I stood up and watched as he and two nurses, both with red, tearful eyes, worked on Mama. After a few minutes, he waved them off and looked up at me.

"I am sorry, Daystar. I can't do anything for her."

I barely heard him. I stared at Mama.

"I know her daughter," I said numbly.

"She should be told," he said, and I nodded, unable to take my eyes off of her.

I forced myself to stand, and then I walked out on shaking legs and took off into the sky. I landed on the roof of a nearby office building and emptied my stomach, falling to my knees as my stomach heaved and my nose ran and I cried harder than I ever thought it was possible to cry. And then I screamed, long, and loud, and even to me, to what was left in me, I sounded like a wounded animal of some kind, screeching my agony over the streets and the blissfully clueless people who traveled them.

I stayed on my knees, that final image of my mother all I could see.

And then it was replaced by another image. Dr. Death's calm, snide face as I watched my mother take her last breaths.

I got up and flew toward Command. I would get some answers. And I didn't care anymore what it took to get them.

*Part Two*
*Wrath*

# CHAPTER THIRTEEN

I arrived at Command and walked through the flight bay entrance without acknowledging any of the people I passed. I maintained my stony silence down the elevator, through the lobby, and into the prison wing. I stormed through the men's wing. I knew Maddoc wouldn't know anything. No, Daemon had always been the one who'd seemed closest to Dr. Death. I let myself into his cell, and he sat in his chair, watching me.

I didn't say anything for a few moments, not wanting him to hear my voice shake. Not wanting to cry. Not now. I swallowed.

"You are going to get one chance here. Just one, and if you don't answer, the pain will start. Don't fuck with me because I'm really not in the mood."

He didn't say anything, just sat there watching me.

"Where can I find Dr. Death?"

"Ugh, this again," he said, shaking his head. "Don't you people ever come up with any original material?"

I waited a beat, and then I sent an energy punch at his face. His head rocked back into the headrest, and I heard his nose crunch. I watched as he shouted in pain, as blood gushed down his face.

"Let's try that again. Where can I find Dr. Death?"

"Fuck you," he shouted.

"Wrong answer." I sent another punch at him, this time an uppercut to his jaw. His head snapped back sharply, and I heard his teeth snap together. He shouted, then moaned in agony.

"Where can I find Dr. Death?"

"I don't know!"

I took a breath, and hit him again.

"Are you scared yet?" I asked him, echoing the words he'd said to me when we'd first brought him in, smug little snot. "Because you should be."

His eyes were wide, his face a mask of rage and pain.

"Where can I find— "

"He has an apartment downtown! In the Westin building on Shelby. Jesus Christ, lady," he begged.

"What is the apartment number? What floor?"

"Penthouse," he said.

Just then, Portia and Jenson hurried into the room, asking me in loud tones what the hell was going on.

"Keep your fucking mouth shut now," I told him. I shoved past my teammates and stormed through the hallways to the nearest flight bay, and I took off toward Shelby.

Movement. Action. It would keep me from falling apart. I could do that later. Or not. All that mattered now is getting vengeance for my mother's death.

I thought of her house, nearly perfect, sitting there empty, and I almost lost it. I forced the thought back and brought my focus back where it needed to be.

Vengeance.

Payback.

The Westin came into view. The penthouse had two large balconies, one looking out over the river, one looking toward the skyscrapers downtown. I landed on the balcony near the river and sent a blast of power at the French doors. They shattered, blowing inward with the impact.

I just caught sight of Death running down a hallway, and I stormed after him. I shoved my way through the closed doorway at the end of the hall, and I heard a gun start firing, over and over agin. Some automatic bullshit. I felt several impacts, but kept stalking forward, trusting that my body armor would do its job. And he wasn't a very good shot. He was shouting, screaming. Begging.

I hated him more for that. My mother never would have stooped to begging. I stepped forward and grabbed him by the front of the throat. "Time to come out and play, doctor," I snarled.

He held up his other hand, the one not holding a gun, and blew something into my face. I was distracted by the acrid odor, the way my eyes started stinging, and it was enough for him to wrench his way free of my grip. I quickly turned on my mask's air filtering components and tried to catch my breath. Whatever it had been, it was nasty shit. I swore I could feel my throat closing up, and every breath brought a stinging pain in my nose and throat. My eyes continued to water as I stumbled out of the room and down the hallway back toward the living room. He had his phone in his hand, in the middle of dialing.

"What the hell are you?" he muttered, shoving it back in his pocket. He picked up another gun, and as he started shooting at me I had to wonder how many of them he had stashed around the place. This one was bigger, stronger, and each bullet that hit my body armor threw me back a little bit.

Not enough to stop me, but still. And I knew I'd be bruised to hell.

I punched out toward him, and the gun went flying from his hands.

"Poison? Guns? That's all you've got?"

"The poison is my power, you crazy bitch. And you're supposed to be as dead as your mother right now," he snarled. He tried to run, and I punched at him again and he went flying into the dark mahogany book cases at the end of the room. He slumped to the floor and groaned. I walked across the room and picked him up by the front of the throat, lifting him high into the air.

And then I started walking.

"Put me down. Stop. Help!" he shouted, and I rolled my eyes as I moved toward the windows. "Please, for the love of god just stop," he begged, sounding every bit like the slime ball he was. I wordlessly carried him through the living room, to the windows. And then I threw him, the sound of shattering glass punctuated by his terrified screams as he started falling fifty-some stories.

I jumped through after him and flew, catching him about halfway down.

"Do you really think you're getting off that easily?" I asked, and he begged some more.

I tried to think of where I could stash him while I dealt with Mama's funeral arrangements. Wayne State's campus caught my eye, and I had an idea. I flew him toward the freeway, toward the off-ramp, to the row of rundown houses that still stood there. At the end of the block stood the charred remains of the house Darla, my little firestarter friend, had once lived in. I swung around, then landed in one of the barren, empty lots behind it. I clamped a hand over Death's mouth and shoved him, hard, into the gaping back door of the house. He tried to scurry away from me, and I kicked him hard in the ribs. He tried to get up again, and I tossed power at him, catching his ribs again. He landed with an "oof" and a pained groan.

"How are your ribs?" I mimicked, throwing his snide words after I'd nearly had him near the waterfront back at him. He stayed down while I rifled through the pouches on my belt. An emergency dampener, which was barebones — it dampened but didn't track, which was perfect. I didn't want anyone else finding him yet. I activated it, then pulled out a roll of heavy duty tape and placed three strong pieces over his mouth. I tied his ankles together with some thin but very strong rope we kept on hand, and then I used the electro cuffs we usually used to secure prisoners for transport. I pulled his hands behind his back, around a sturdy steel pillar, then I secured the cuffs.

I spotted his phone peeking out of his jacket pocket, and I grabbed it and stuck it in my pouch. "I'll be back in a bit, and you and I are going to have a little chat. Right now, I have to arrange to bury my mother."

I took a breath, then I looked toward him again.

"You're going to pay dearly for that, by the way. Don't try to get free. I'll get an alert the second the cuffs pick up any signs of attempted escape, and I if you think you're in pain now, you're going to be in absolute agony if I have to come back here before I'm ready. Understand?"

He nodded. Wide-eyed. I watched him in disgust, worthless maggot that he was, and then I walked out the back door and flew back toward Command. I needed to change into normal clothes, and then I needed to make funeral arrangements for Mama.

I didn't even know where to start.

# CHAPTER FOURTEEN

I arrived at Command a little while later and made my way down to the team lounge. This time of day, everyone was kind of between shifts, and I had a feeling they'd all been called back after Portia and Jenson had seen me apparently go nuts on Daemon. I walked into the lounge, and they were all there. The quiet chatter stopped, and they all looked at me. Portia was about to say something, when I held my hand up.

"My mother is dead," I said quietly. Jenson, David, and Ryan stood up.

"What?" Portia asked in a hushed tone, hands at her mouth.

"Four o'clock. The thing that would happen if I didn't deliver. He murdered my mother at four o'clock today. Put poison in her coffee, then called me. I got to watch her die via video call. By the time I got there, she was already gone."

I delivered it all in a monotone.

"Oh my god," Chance whispered. Amy patted her shoulder. Portia still stood there, looking shocked. Jenson came to me and pulled me into her arms.

"I'm sorry. I'm so sorry, Jolene," she whispered, holding me tight. I hugged her back.

"So. I need to change. And then I need to go to make arrangements... I don't even know what the hell I'm supposed to be doing," I said, and I started to feel my control give way.

"It's okay. I'll go with you," Jenson said. "Okay?"

I looked at her blankly. She had tears in her eyes, and that was when I lost it. I cried in great, heaving gulps, and Jenson held me as I cried. I felt someone pat my shoulder, and then a large, warm hand rubbing my back as David and Ryan tried to comfort me.

I managed to pull myself together, and I patted Jenson's back and pulled away. "I can't do this now," I said, sniffling.

"You have every right to do this now," Ryan said.

I shook my head. "Not now. Now is for giving my mother a proper burial and bringing her killer to justice."

"That's why you were in there with Daemon. Did he tell you anything?" Portia asked.

I thought for a second, then shook my head. "He didn't know. Did he tell you all anything after I left?"

"Not a word," Jenson said angrily.

"Okay. So I have work to do. I'm going to go change."

"I'll drive. I'll meet you in the lobby in ten, okay?" Jenson said, and I nodded.

I changed into jeans and a dark gray sweater, hastily ran a brush through my hair, then went down to the lobby, where Jenson was already waiting. For once, she looked less than perfectly put together, as if she'd grabbed the first items she's put her hands on, which were a rumpled pair of jeans and a faded Navy t-shirt. She put her arm around me, drawing me in for a quick hug before we started walking toward the elevator down to the parking garage. Once we got there, she went to the far side of the area, which was where those of us on the team who kept our own cars for times like this stored them. She unlocked an older model Jeep Wrangler and we got in.

"Which funeral home do you want to have handle this?" she asked as she started it up.

I looked at her blankly. "I have no idea. Um. I think the closest one to where we lived was Pearson's over by Masonic."

She glanced at the dashboard clock. "It's only five thirty. We'll go over there and see if we can talk to somebody and get things moving. Was she active in church? Do you want a funeral mass or anything like that?"

I shook my head. "She wasn't really a church person."

"Okay. So just the funeral home, then." We drove in silence for a while. "She was a lovely lady. While you were in the medical wing after the Maddoc thing, we chatted quite a bit. And she thought Caine was hot," she added with a small smile, and I let out a little laugh, which seemed wrong.

"She never mentioned that part," I said, blinking back tears.

"Something about his backside," she said, glancing over at me, and I shook my head. She reached over and squeezed my hand, then put both hands back on the wheel.

We drove most of the way to the funeral home in silence, and, when we got there, we were ushered to a quiet office where a solemn little woman took me through the process. I picked out a coffin, gravestone, memorial card. I signed a bunch of stuff, authorizing this or that.

"We'll have the body transported from Detroit Receiving," she said. "You'll need to choose clothing for her to wear." She glanced at a computer on her desk. "Do you want a day for people to come and visit her here, or just a viewing before the funeral procession."

"Just on the day of the funeral is fine," I said. I felt numb.

"So we can plan on it for the day after tomorrow, then," the woman said. "Is that all right?"

I nodded. I signed more things, and then Jenson and I left.

"If you have family and stuff to contact, I can help with that," she said after we got into the car. I shook my head. "

It was just us. Her neighbors will want to come, though, and her friends from work if they can manage to get it off."

"Do you want a wake after the funeral?"

I looked at her blankly.

"A luncheon for everyone to get together afterward," she said gently.

"Oh, right. I guess we should do that."

"I have a cousin who owns a restaurant in St. Clair Shores. I'm sure I can work it out with him so we can have it there."

"Really?"

She nodded. "Just give me the go ahead, and I'll handle that part if you want."

"You are a lifesaver," I said, and she shook her head.

"I wish I could do more."

"You're here," I said.

I spent the rest of the night shopping for a burial outfit for Mama and dropping it off at the funeral home, then going to the trailer park and talking to Mama's neighbors. Just about all of them cried, but I was numb, and I couldn't shake it. I kept thinking of Dr. Death sitting in that house. It would just have to wait. Right now if he got away, it wasn't exactly my biggest concern. I'd find him again, and there would be no getting away a second time. If David's electro cuffs were functioning the way they should be, he hadn't tried to get away. I hadn't gotten any alerts, but the component that tracked his pulse and temperature indicated that he was pretty stressed out. Good.

After I finished running around, I called Mama's department at work and spoke to one of her friends, Marianne, who I'd met a few times. They already knew she was gone, of course, so at least I didn't have to deal with sobs of shock. I relayed the funeral information, and she told me there were a lot of people who wanted to come. She also took the name of the funeral home.

Jenson stopped by my room to tell me that the wake was all set, and I thanked her. She left, sensing that I wanted to be alone. I sat on the floor in front of the floor-to-ceiling windows in my living room, looking over the dark city without seeing it. Part of me wanted to have a chat with Dr. Death right that instant, but I knew that, if I confronted him now, I'd kill him. I'd do it without a second thought, and in the end, it wouldn't do anything. My mother had died for the stupid injection he was obsessed with making. She'd died over his power trip, over some insane plan to put his team of villainous assholes in charge. I needed to know how far he'd gotten. I needed to destroy every last piece of what he'd been working toward. I needed to know who was involved, besides the obvious Mayhem assholes, if anyone. I needed to make sure that every last person involved in Mama's death paid. And while killing him would make me feel a hell of a lot better, it wasn't nearly punishment enough. Mama would have wanted the world kept safe from whatever his endgame had been. I could do that much, I hoped.

I sat, and I stared, and I thought. I watched the sky darken, then watched it lighten again, going from black to midnight blue, blue to thunderous gray, and then gray gave way to a golden rosiness that seemed out of place.

Eventually, I made myself get up, shower, and pull the uniform on. I looked at my mask, remembering the way Death had tried to attack me the day before. My throat still burned, and my eyes were swollen. I think that was more due to crying, though, than anything Death had tried.

*What the hell are you?*

I wasn't anything, other than someone who was so pissed off at the time that I wasn't about to let anything stop me from getting a hold of him.

I pulled my mask back on, then my boots and gloves, and I made it to the flight bay just in time to catch Ryan.

Amy had offered to fill in for me, and I refused. I wanted to work. It was that or sit around until I felt calm enough to confront Death without killing him. Doing something productive would help some in that regard.

So I did my usual patrol route with Ryan, despite everyone telling me to take some time off. We mostly didn't talk, and I was grateful that he didn't try to force the issue. I actually considered taking him with me when I talked to Death, to keep me from going too far, but then I realized that this was personal now. It was between Death and me, at least for now, and I wanted the first crack at him. I wanted to hear him tell me what about his stupid little plan had been so important that it had been worth killing an innocent woman for.

When our shift ended, Ryan and I took the elevator together down from the flight bay.

"We'll all be there tomorrow, you know," he said quietly.

I glanced over at him. "You guys didn't know her."

"Well, we all met her. But even if we hadn't, we'd be there anyway. You're one of us," he added with a shrug. I hadn't expected any of them to come. Jenson, probably, and maybe David, but the idea that they were all coming was news to me.

"Thanks," I said, and he gave a short nod.

"You know, if there's anything you need, I'm here. Right?"

"I know."

"Give me something to do for you, Jolene," he said quietly. "Name it."

I was going to tell him there was nothing, and then I remembered what the woman at the funeral home mentioned, something I'd tried not to think about too much.

"Actually…"

"What?"

"Um. The funeral home lady said I might want to ask for pallbearers ahead of time. We don't really have any male family members. It's okay if you don't want to— "

He reached out and took my hand. "I can definitely do that. If you want, I can ask David, too. That will be two of the six, then."

I nodded. "That would be great. I think with you two and then maybe our old neighbors, that would do it." I looked up at him. "Thanks."

"Sure."

"I'm going to go flying for a while, I think. Try to clear my head a little."

He nodded, and once he got off on his floor, I took the elevator back up to the top flight deck.

I took off toward Midtown, flying in cloudy, gray sky, which fit my mood and state of mind just fine. Time to check and see if I'd scared Dr. Death enough to stay. And, more, if I'd scared him enough to make him talk.

If not, I would just have to try harder.

# CHAPTER FIFTEEN

I landed in the open field behind where Darla's family's burned out house was. I could hear the traffic roaring by on I-94. It was cloudy, and the air carried that heaviness, that oppressive sense of fullness that it always had just before it rained. I ducked between empty houses until I got to the blackened shell of the house I'd stashed Death in. I walked through the back door and he was still there, cuffed, as he had been, to the pillar. The handcuffs had worked the way they were supposed to. I'd have to congratulate David next time I saw him.

He stared up at me, making noises behind the duct tape covering his mouth. I leaned over him and wrenched it off, and he gave a shout of pain. He smelled of piss and sweat.

"Okay. I have to bury my mother tomorrow morning, so I'm really not in the mood to fuck around with you. Don't tempt me, because if you thought that what I did to you yesterday hurt, you really don't want to see what happens when I'm in a little more control."

He was breathing fast, hard, looking up at me in horror.

"So you need to tell me about this formula you were working on. How close is it to being done? Has it been tested on anyone? How is it supposed to work? And why were you so fucking obsessed with me?"

He didn't answer at first, and I drew my fist back. He flinched.

"Okay! Okay. It was close enough to done, but to be as powerful as we wanted, we needed your sample to incorporate into the formula. It's nothing to do with you personally. You're just the strongest super powered person as far as anyone knows, so your sample would have increased the powers of anyone injected."

"So it was an injection," I said, reaffirming what David and Jenson had already discovered.

"Yes. I initially wanted something I could distribute as a gas like I did in Midtown, but we all saw how well that worked. That was just a trial. The final product required your sample, and that taught me that it doesn't work well. As an injection, though…" he gave a nod. "That works."

"So it has been tested on people?"

"There have been three tests. One was successful. I built from there." I was somewhat surprised by how openly he was speaking, but then I realized that it fit with what I knew of Dr. Death. He loved to talk about himself. Self-absorbed jackass. And he was probably hoping that it would save him, if he talked. Because I could see in his eyes that he expected me to kill him.

Hell, *I* expected me to kill him.

"You were working with Alpha," I said.

"Yes."

"Why?"

"We had partnerships with high ranking members of many teams. Alpha was just one of them. And I think it's obvious why: it made it very easy to get a wide range of samples. Yours was the only one we had any trouble with, which is why I was ordered to do what I did."

I opened my mouth to talk, and then I shook my head. "You are such a fucking weasel. You killed my mother while I watched— "

"You think that was my idea?" he asked, raising his voice. "How often do you see me do something so publicly? I hate behavior like that. So crass."

I stared at him, and he laughed. Just shook his head and laughed.

"It's your team," I pressed. He was going to take responsibility for this. He wasn't going to weasel out of it.

"It was never my team," he sneered. "All I ever wanted was a big payday and the ability to work uninterrupted as often as I wanted. I finally had it. I provided the lab and the intelligence. Mayhem kept the super hero teams busy while we worked on other things. I was more than happy to spend all of my time in my lab. I kept meticulous track of the process. It was beautiful. Notebooks and notebooks worth of it," he said in a wistful voice.

"Isn't that kind of archaic? I'm pretty sure most of that happens on computes."

"Computers can be hacked, as we well know thanks to Virus. And I didn't trust him in particular. He was too close, too loyal to you."

"He told you where to find my mother," I realized.

"No."

"No?"

He shrugged.

I shook my head and tried to re-focus on what I was supposed to be finding out. "Where's the lab, Death? Where's the data?"

He opened his mouth, and surprised look came over his face. Then I saw the tip of a sword suddenly poke through his chest. I looked behind him, into the shadows.

"You talk too fuckin' much," a too-familiar voice said, rough, just a hint of Scottish brogue. The sword receded, and Connor stepped out of the shadows, dressed, as usual, head-to-toe in black.

I stared as he wiped the blade on Death's jacket then held the sword at his side. He raised his face, and I knew he was looking at me.

I felt bile rise in my throat.

*I'll try to keep an eye on your mom for you.* Words I'd once taken as evidence that he maybe cared for me. That he understood me. My knees wanted to buckle, and all I could do was stare at him.

"I did give you a chance to be a good girl," he said. For an instant, I wished I could see his face, to make all of this more real. But in the same moment, I realized how that would just make it all worse, somehow. "But I knew you were too stubborn to take advantage of it."

I tried to shake myself out of the crazy, panicky feeling coursing through me.

He kept talking. "At the same time, we both know that your mother was the only thing keeping you from what you could be, if you'd get your head out of your ass and wake up. So concerned with making your Mama proud," he said with derision. "You belong by my side. In every way."

"You...." I couldn't finish.

"Me," he said. "I needed your blood. It was the last step toward making my plans a reality." He looked at Death's still form. "Now I have to find a new scientist. Fuck," he said. "See? You make everything so fucking difficult, Jolene."

"This is my fault?" I asked. I felt like I could hardly breathe.

"I needed your blood. But I need you, too. The two of us, sweetheart. Just think about how much we could do. Nothing could stand against us."

"You are insane. You're fucking delusional. You murdered my mother, you absolute son of a bitch," I said, my voice rising. I drew my fist back and sent a punch of power at him, and he flew through the house, crashing through the opposite exterior wall into the empty yard outside. I stormed after him. He sprang up and launched at me, swords hissing through the air. I jumped back, then sent another punch at him.

"Impressive," he said. "When'd you learn how to do that?" I punched again, and he went flying through the air. He bounced back up and stormed toward me, faster than should have been possible. Faster than I remember him being able to move.

And then it hit me. I should have known he was there. The house wasn't that dark inside, that he could completely stay obscured by the shadows. He'd been invisible before he'd killed Death. The other samples Alpha had undoubtedly sent him would have included Crystal's sample. Invisibility.

He'd been the success that Death had mentioned.

He swung again, and I flew up into the air.

"Get back here. We're not done yet." And then he rose into the air, too, and I wanted to scream. I flew toward the freeway, trying to get some distance to figure out what the hell to do. He was bigger than me. Had a healing factor, which made him really hard to hurt enough to slow him down. Plus he apparently had a crazy soup of a bunch of other powers thanks to Death's injection.

"Ah, ah, ah. Get your ass back here," he shouted, his deep raspy voice sending chills down my spine. Not the way it once had. Once, it had been a pleasant chill. Excitement. This… this was terror. "Look," he shouted. He lifted his wrist to his mouth and said something, just as I noticed that StrikeForce had appeared in the yard where we'd been fighting. And, at that moment, a second team appeared. I was able to make out a few villains I knew of. A Russian guy who called himself "Red Scare," a guy from Britain known as "Plague" and a chick from Japan that I think was calling herself "Flame" or some shit like that. I looked at Connor.

"I figured they'd want to come and help you," he said. "They're becoming a complication I don't need. But you're worth the complications you give me."

"Are you kidding me?" I punched out at him again, and again, and again. He went flailing across the sky. I tried to keep an eye on StrikeForce as I got ready to hit him again. He'd keep healing, but maybe if I hit him hard enough I could knock him out. It would be enough, maybe, to get a dampener on him.

Assuming, of course, that my teammates had remembered to bring one. Or a dozen, based on the crowd he'd ordered into place. How the hell had they gotten there so fast?

Of course. He'd moved them into place, because he probably had Portia or Brianne's powers too, that same ability to transport.

He flew toward me, brandishing his swords, and I punched out at him. I vaguely noticed news helicopters circling nearby, traffic stopped on the freeway below us. It was raining harder now, fat drops that splattered against my uniform when they hit.

I lost track of how many times I sent blasts of power at him, how many times I ducked his blades. How many times I felt a blade scrape across my body armor. This wasn't working, I realized with more than a little terror. A quick glance below me, in the lots around Darla's house, showed, to my surprise, that my team seemed to be holding their own. David was facing off against two of Raider's people, back to back with Steel, who was in her metallic form and keeping three of the baddies off of David's back. Screamer was doing her thing, and five of the villains were clutching their heads. As she kept screaming, their agony got worse, and Toxxin went around, easily and quickly putting them down with her powers. Portia and Jenson were taking on Raider (the current Raider, Connor's ex-wife) and two of her henchmen.

Holy shit. We were winning, I realized. I saw some of the others, including a few of the more powerful guards from the prison, who were going around quickly and efficiently collaring the baddies that lay there unconscious.

I flew away from Connor.

"I'm getting bored with this game, sweetheart," he shouted. I needed to do something now, while StrikeForce had the upper hand, which, in and of itself, was practically a miracle.

I dove, fast and hard, right at him. He was so used to me hitting him from afar that I think it took him by surprise when I rocketed toward him. I smashed into Connor and he went flying, falling, his swords clattering to the ground on the freeway below. I'd stunned him. Now I had to make sure he stayed down.

I stayed with him, and it came to me. This was when I had to try to use the things Ryan had taught me, all of that wrestling shit I thought I'd never have to use once we discovered how my body compensated for my messed up reflexes. I knew any move trying to hold him would fail, because he was so much bigger than me. But everyone has pressure points. Even him.

And his uniform isn't padded at the throat, I realized, remembering the way it looked when he rolled it up to kiss me. I shook the memory away.

We landed in a heap on the side of the freeway, and I moved as quickly as I could. I dug my fingers into the side of his neck, hard. Someone with my strength, someone who's been trained to incapacitate someone this way, even against someone of Connor's size... It was almost frightening how easy it actually was. He slumped to the ground within seconds.

"Bring one of those collars over here," I called, hoping one of the prison guards would hear me.

"Oh, shit. He's down, he's down," I heard one of the baddies shouting, terror in his voice. "Fall back. Fall the fuck back. Pick him up." I looked around, keeping a hand wrapped around his wrist, making sure I didn't lose contact with him.

"I need a collar," I shouted as I felt him start stirring. I went to hit his pressure point again, and suddenly, he was just gone. Not invisible, but actually gone. I noticed, almost at the same instant, that the sounds of battle had ended as well. I looked around in a panicked frenzy, then rose into the air to see my team looking confused where they'd been battling. Every one of our opponents was gone.

"What the hell was that?" Ryan growled. "What's going on?"

"He wanted you guys here. To get ambushed by his people."

"That was Killjoy," Jenson said, confused, and I nodded. She stared at me. "Killjoy?" she repeated, and all I could do was stand there, just as confused as she was. Maybe more.

They all looked stunned. Confused. Pissed. And I felt pretty much the same way, with the additional sense of being a complete, absolute fool.

"We better get back. Come on," Portia said woodenly. We gathered around, and she teleported us to the meeting room at Command.

# CHAPTER SIXTEEN

Once we appeared back at Command it only took us a second to realize that there were alarms sounding, and we ran out of the meeting room. It was all eerily quiet. No one moving around on the upper administrative floors. We made our way down to the main lobby, and that was where we saw the first signs that something was horribly wrong. The woman who'd taken Jenson's place at the receptionist's desk was on the floor. Jenson went over to her, then breathed, a look of relief on her face.

"She's alive," she said. We saw more bodies near the prison wing, and I flew in that direction, the rest of the team behind me.

I could see from the blood that these people probably hadn't made it. The door to the women's wing stood open, and my eyes went to a prone figure on the floor in front of an open cell.

"No, no, no," I muttered. I came to a landing next to Marie. Her eyes were open, and she was still. I checked for a pulse, knowing I wouldn't find one. I glanced toward the open cell. I knew before I looked whose it would be. Brianne. The transporter from Dr. Death's…. Connor's team. She was gone.

I looked back at Marie. She'd been kind to me when she'd been my prison guard. She'd helped us stage our little uprising, and she'd become a friend. I gently closed her eyes, then shook my head and took off for the men's prison wing.

There was more carnage there. My team was gathered at the far end, and someone was sobbing. I raced there, unsurprised, now, to see Maddoc and Daemon's cells empty. I glanced toward where Alpha and Nightbane were held, and noted that they were both in their cells.

They truly had pissed Connor off, I guess. When I got to my teammates, I found Dani sobbing over someone on the floor.

"Oh, Christ," I breathed. Monica lay on the floor in a pool of blood. My knees finally gave out on me then, and I sank to the floor, unable to tear my eyes away from Monica but seeing, instead, Mama lying there.

I couldn't breath. I started shaking, and I covered my mouth with my hands, afraid that I'd either sob or vomit and not feeling like adding to the insanity by doing either of them. Amy knelt next to Dani, her arm around her shoulders, and Dani rested her head on Amy's shoulder as she cried. Portia stood there like a statue. David and Jenson stood together, neither of them looking, for once, like they knew what to do next.

I just kept shaking. I jumped when I felt a strong arm around my waist.

"Okay. It's okay," Ryan said quietly as he pulled me up off the floor.

"How did you guys decide to come there today?" I asked him, determined to pull myself together at least a little.

"We got a bunch of anonymous tips that you and Dr. Death had been seen there, and that there were other villains around. So we went, figuring you'd need back up. When we got there, we didn't see anything at first, other than you and Killjoy."

I closed my eyes. "He wanted to draw you guys out of here. This was part of the plan," I said softly. "David and Jenson," I said.

"Yeah?" David asked.

"Can you guys go over the security footage? I want to see who he sent in to do this." I already had a sinking feeling that I knew at least one of them, realizing that someone had been missing from our battle by the freeway.

David and Jenson nodded, then left, David patting Dani's shoulder as he passed, Jenson leaning down and hugging her quickly before stepping away.

I spent the afternoon helping to put things somewhat back to normal. Portia was locked in her office with Amy and Dani, making burial arrangements, while Ariana, Ryan, and Chance worked with me organizing the med staff and fielding questions from StrikeForce employees who had been in other parts of the building at the time. I was just grateful, at this point, that they'd been focused on particular people, not mass slaughter. I remembered what Jenson had said, that in a world where people had super strength, someone with her low-level powers didn't stand a chance. That was true for most of those who worked at StrikeForce.

Once things were somewhat calmed down, I made my way to David's lab. He and Jenson were looking at the monitors over his desk.

"So. Lemme guess. Virus," I said, and they nodded.

I closed my eyes, fighting back the nausea trying to come over me, the rage I had at myself. One more person in an ever-growing list of people I stupidly trusted once upon a time.

"Did he have help?" I asked. Jenson nodded toward the screen, and I watched. He'd come in with two guys. The first one used some kind of telekinetic powers to toss the receptionist across the room, and they left her lying where she landed. They made their way to the prison wing. The first guy kept tossing people out of their way, but the second did some weird little wave with his hand, and slices opened across throats.

"That's Render," David said quietly. "Until now, we all assumed he was dead. No one's seen him in over a year."

We watched as the first kinetic guy went after Marie. She was trying to block them out of Brianne's cell, and he threw her. Her head hit one of the walls, and she went down. I watched as Virus started moving his hands, a movement, a gesture I knew well from when we'd worked together. Brianne's door slid open, and, after a bit more gesturing from Virus, her manacles opened and she joined the group of villains, smiling and talking as they made their way out of the women's wing, and toward the men's wing.

I didn't want to watch the moment Monica died, but I felt, in some weird way, that it was the least I owed her. I watched as the villains marched in, taking down guards as they did. Monica stood at the end of the hall. She used her powers to throw the kinetic back and into Render. They both stumbled, and she threw Virus at them. That happened three or four times. Every time they got up, she did it again, and I realized, sickeningly, that she was trying to buy time.

That she assumed we were coming to help her.

"Why weren't we alerted?"

"Communications systems were all fried. They probably signaled for help right away," Jenson said.

I watched her throw the kinetic again, and then a large red slice opened across her throat, and another down her chest, and she fell to the floor. It only took moments for Virus to get Daemon and Maddoc out, all of them laughing, shaking hands. They started walking out, and as they passed the camera, Maddoc looked up, grinned, and mouthed the words, "Later, Daystar."

A small sound escaped me, and I barely refrained from blasting the monitor. I dug Dr. Death's phone, which I'd hung onto since taking him, out of my pocket. "I know tracing calls can be tricky. Can you trace where this has been though? Some kind of internal GPS thing? Is that how it works?"

David nodded. "That shouldn't be a problem. Gimme a minute." He took the phone from me and hooked it up to one of his computers. Jenson looked at me questioningly.

"I'm working on something."

She nodded and let it go.

"There's some extra security on here. I think I can crack it, but it'll take longer than I thought. Maybe by tonight," he said. I looked at him, at the dark circles under his eyes, the bruises on his face from the fight.

"Get some rest. Work on it when you can," I said.

David watched me for a minute. "I'll rest later." I nodded, then turned and left.

I took the elevator up to my floor, then let myself into my suite. I glanced at my phone automatically checking to see if Mama had called while I was out, then remembered that she was gone. I sank down onto the couch and stared into the darkness of my suite. If there wasn't anything I could use on that phone, this had all come to nothing. Worse than nothing, because now we'd lost some of our people and we had to track our three former prisoners down again.

I leaned my head back against the couch and closed my eyes. I'd spent all day either trying not to think about what I had to do the next day or dealing with the chaos that Connor...Connor! I couldn't think about that now... had brought into my life. But now I was alone and nobody needed me, and all I could think about was that tomorrow I'd have to see my mother in a coffin. I'd have to listen to well-wishers say how sorry they were. I'd have to sit through a meal after laying Mama to rest.

I didn't feel strong enough to do any of it. And the thing was, there wasn't any other way to look at the fact that her death was my fault. I'd trusted Connor, not questioned him when he told me he knew where Mama lived. I'd gotten involved in this superhero shit, ignored his demands. If I'd done just one of those things differently, Mama would still be alive.

He was going to pay. And it was going to hurt. But it wouldn't change the fact that me and my shitty judgment when it comes to people was a pretty direct cause of Mama's murder.

"I'm sorry, Mama," I whispered into my empty suite. I drifted off, and I don't know how long I was asleep when I woke with a start, taking a minute to realize that Jenson's voice was talking to me over my comm.

"What. What? I was asleep," I said groggily.

"He cracked it," she said, and I jumped up. I got down to his lab as quickly as I could. They both greeted me, looking exhausted. David pointed to a map on the large monitor in front of him. There were several red dots on the map, of varying sizes.

"The larger the dot, the more often the phone was there, right?" I asked, and he nodded.

There was a large red dot over Detroit, which made sense. A few smaller dots elsewhere in the midwest and in Britain and Scotland.

And then there was a large red dot over what looked like an island off the coast of Mexico.

"What's that? Can we get a satellite image of that?"

David nodded and after a moment, a sat image popped up. He zoomed in, showing a nondescript concrete building, roughly square. No windows. A chainlink fence and a single driveway leading up to the front door and parking lot.

"You're a miracle worker. Thank you," I said to David, and he shook his head, even if he did end up looking pleased. "Thanks, both of you. Now go get some rest." I took the phone with me, unplugging it from David's computer, then made my way up to Portia's office. She was just coming out when I got there.

"I need to talk to you," I said.

She turned to look at me. Her eyes were bloodshot, with dark circles beneath them.

"It can wait. You don't have to deal with this now," she said gently.

"No. I really do. I found something, and I feel like I owe you some information about Killjoy."

She opened her office back up again and walked in. I followed her, and we sat down on opposite sides of her desk.

I started by filling her in on how things started between me and Killjoy. And, later, what he'd told me about his days of Raider. How I'd decided to stop seeing him and how his persistence had been both annoying and scary, all at once. And then I told her about the moment he stepped out of the shadows and killed Dr. Death.

"I thought I'd lost my mind. That I couldn't possibly be seeing what I was seeing. At first, I thought, maybe he was trying to save me from Death or something, you know? Maybe he was still on my side. And then he started talking. He's been behind it all along. The emails, forming Mayhem, working with Alpha... all of it."

She sat there, looking pale, her face drawn and tense. "I never pictured anything like this when I agreed to lead this team," she finally said. "I am so sorry, Jolene. I can't even imagine what you're feeling. I feel like I've landed in an alien world with no map and no clue how to speak the language."

I nodded. It wasn't a bad comparison. All it needed was the addition of soul-crushing loss, and she was dead on.

"There's more," I said.

"Of course there is."

I went over what Jenson and David had found when they'd cracked the files, and she knew most of it, that Death was making a formula dealing with powers, and that Alpha had made a deal to give him samples from StirkeForce. "So when I had Death, he told me that they need my sample, and I kept refusing to give it to them, and they ended up...

well, you know," I said, unable to say the words, "to punish me."

She nodded and put her hand on mine, leaning over the desk.

"Anyway. They were making this, with this overall scheme of ultimately controlling world governments, building their own superhero army. I assumed this was all Death's idea."

"And it was really Killjoy's," she said softly. I nodded.

"Before Killjoy killed him, Death told me that the formula and all of his notes were in a lab, one Death worked at all the time. He kept handwritten records. There are no computer files or anything like that, because he was paranoid that someone else would end up with his research if he kept it digitally. So if we can find and destroy this facility, this lab, that puts an end to Killjoy's little injected army plot."

She was watching me. "And? Did you find it?"

"I tracked the location from Death's phone's GPS." I left David and Jenson out of it. She didn't need to know that they'd been helping me all along. "The lab is located just off the coast of Mexico. We go there, we destroy everything, we arrest whoever is there, and we hurt him. Bad."

She sat thinking for a few moments, then shook her head sadly. "It's not that simple."

"What do you mean? Yes it is."

"You're talking about going to an island in international territory and destroying it and arresting people who may not even be American citizens."

"This has to be stopped."

"It would cause an international incident," she said. "And trust of superheroes is already at a major low. We can't go marching or flying or whatever into a foreign country and just start breaking stuff."

"So, what? We just sit here and let it happen?"

"I'll take it to the international tribunal." I started arguing, and she talked over me. "StirkeForce can't make a move until we have their support. We do, we're immediately on everyone's bad side. We're hanging on by a thread here. I know you want to make them pay, but we need to go through the proper channels."

I still had my mouth open to argue, and I clamped it shut.

"Email me the information you have, and I'll present it. Okay?" Portia asked.

"Fine."

"Okay. I'm sorry. I know you wanted a different answer, but— "

"I understand," I said.

She nodded. "Okay. Let's get some rest."

We got up, and she patted my shoulder. We rode the elevator down to our floor together.

"She was a really nice lady," Portia said as we stepped off the elevator.

"She was," I said.

"She was proud of you."

I met her eyes then. "Well. That was a mistake, huh? Considering that someone I stupidly trusted killed her."

"Jolene."

I waved her off and let myself into my suite. I paced and thought.

And a few minutes later, I had changed out of my uniform and was out, flying toward Hamtramck.

I'd tried handling this the official way. Now it was time to handle it my way.

I landed in a park, looked around to make sure nobody was around, which wasn't likely due to the late hour and the rain, which had been falling since our fight against Killjoy's team. It felt like a month ago, at least, with all that had happened since.

I shoved my hands into the pockets of my black jacket and walked down the street toward the big old house I'd visited so often, it felt almost like a second home. I went around to the back door, rather than standing under the porch light at the front door. I knocked on the back door quietly. A few moments later, I saw the kitchen light turn on, and then Luther's face peered out the window at me. A second later, I heard the locks clicking, and then she opened the door.

"Didn't expect to see you here again, *kotka*," she said in her scratchy voice.

"I was thinking about you," I said. "I need your advice."

She peered up at me, then held the door open wider. "Come on in. I'll put the tea on."

I sat at the formica table in Luther's yellowed kitchen and watched her shuffle around in her slippers and bathrobe. As I'd always figured, her hair was indeed in curlers and a hairnet. We were silent while she prepared the tea. She placed it on the table, then turned on the radio on the kitchen counter, which was pretty much always, as long as I'd known Luther, set to the sports radio channel. Not because Luther was especially into sports, but because their incessant babble was enough to cover just about any conversation.

I knew she would expect me to speak in code, anyway. I appreciated Luther's distrust of just about everyone even more now than I did when we worked together.

I took a sip of my tea and leaned forward, resting my elbows on the table. "I need to get a gift for someone... special," I said, aware that I was probably not making the most pleasant face. She watched me closely, then nodded.

"What kind of gift? There are all kinds of possibilities. Something to let them know you're thinking of them? Something to keep them warm? Something to feed the stomach?"

I kind of guessed at what she meant. A message or a threat, a little bit of arson, or, I guessed, poison, maybe? It sounded about right.

"Really, I want to get his attention," I said softly, meeting her eyes. I smiled, aware that it was kind of an automatic thing, not something I meant. "Something he couldn't ignore."

She seemed to be thinking.

Then she nodded. "I'll give you this business card I picked up. Lovely little gift shop," she said. "You'll want to be careful. The owner is a little unsure of new customers. I'll let her know to expect you though."

She wrote on the back of a napkin and handed it to me.

"Good luck," she said. "Most of her gift items seem a little overpriced, but how often do you find the perfect thing, yes?"

I nodded, glancing down at the napkin.

"Thanks so much. I knew you'd point me in the right direction."

She smiled then. "Come back anytime, *kotka*. I have missed you."

I got up and she showed me out. I heard the door click locked behind me, then I headed back down the street until I got to the park, where I took off toward the East Side.

I made my way to the neighborhood where my contact had told me to find her and scoped out a good, empty part of the neighborhood to land in. I made my way to a ratty little house just off of Moross. The bell tower of St. Jude church was illuminated in the distance, kind of fuzzy looking through the misty night. I walked up to the front door and knocked. The door opened a minute later, a young woman's face peering out.

"What the fuck do you want?"

"Luther sent me."

She looked me up and down, then nodded. She pulled the door open.

"She mentioned what you wanted. I have a few good options here." She led me into a back bedroom. The house was dark, which made me nervous because if some asshole was hiding in the shadows, I couldn't see them.

"Haven't paid your light bill, huh?"

She snorted. "I don't live in this shit hole. I do business here sometimes. Never bring this shit home with me."

"Good thinking," I said. "Lola, right?"

"That's me. And I wouldn't be here if Luther didn't vouch for you. I never deal with new people."

I didn't answer. I understood that, now better than ever.

She turned around. "Need to see the money first, blondie."

I kept my eyes on her as I reached into my coat pocket. She was short, easily about a half foot shorter than me. Short dark hair, dark eyes, a round face that looked too young to be doing this kind of business. I pressed the wad of bills into her palm and she rifled through it quickly.

"Good." She pocketed it, then went over to the table and pulled what looked like a ratty old Christmas table cloth aside. There were several boxes, different sizes.

"I need something I can use at a distance. Remote," I said.

She shoved two of the items out of the way, leaving three more.

"Either one of these do what you want. You want to get someone's attention? You'll fucking get it."

I looked at the table.

"How much for all three?"

She pulled the wad out of her pocket. "Another one of these."

I dug into my other pocket and pulled out more bills.

She laughed and took them from my hand. "Bitch, they're all yours. Pleasure doing business with you."

"You got a box to put these in?"

She grabbed one from under the table and I loaded it up. We shook quickly, and then I took off just as the sun was starting to rise.

Today was going to be a nightmare. Hopefully, I wouldn't be the only one hurting by the time it was over.

# CHAPTER SEVENTEEN

I rode with Jenson, Ryan, and David in Jenson's Jeep; Ryan and I in the back seat, Jenson and David in front. They argued about the best route to take, and Ryan and I sat silently, each of us watching the view out our respective windows.

For a bunch of second-rate superheroes, we cleaned up pretty well. David and Ryan filled out their black suits nicely, and Jenson wore a suit as well, black pants with a matching jacket. I glanced down at myself, black skirt and a black blouse, and thought how much Mama would have hated all the dark colors.

The funeral home was everything I feared it would be. The same solemn woman who had helped me make the arrangements ushered us into a room with a placard that said "Faraday" outside of the door. I walked in and stood at the back, as close to the doors as I could get without actually stepping out of the room completely. We were a little early, the only four people in the room. The rest of StrikeForce was getting ready to leave when we'd pulled out of the parking garage.

Ryan caught my eye. "Jolene, you'll want to do this before there's an audience," he said quietly, and I shook my head, trying not to look at the coffin.

"He's right," Jenson said softly. "Do you want me to go up with you?"

I shook my head again, then I closed my eyes.

"Let's make sure she gets a minute. Come on," Ryan said to David, and I watched as they went and stood at the entrance of the room, like two bouncers ready to turn away anyone who tried to get in. Jenson patted my arm, and I took another breath and walked up to the coffin. There was a kneeler thing there, beside it, and I knelt on that. I focused on the hardware on the side of the coffin, studiously not looking at Mama. I didn't want to see her like this. This wasn't her. Not anymore. All the life and warmth and humor was gone. I felt tears come to my eyes, and I finally made myself look at her.

She looked like a mannequin in the yellow dress I'd brought for her. Mama rarely wore makeup, and she had far too much on now, I guess to disguise the pallor. Her hair was too curled, too fluffy. Somehow, it made it easier. If she'd looked the way I was used to seeing her, I couldn't have stood it.

"I wish we'd had more time, Mama," I whispered anyway, knowing there were things that needed to be said, and this was the last chance I'd get to see her face while I talked to her. "There's so much I never told you. Too many lies. " I tried to blink back the tears that threatened, and I couldn't. I sniffled. "I was a liar, Mama. And a thief. A con artist. Embezzler. And I'll probably be a lot worse before this is all done." The tears flowed freely now, and I swiped them away angrily. "This is my fault. I should have just done what you wanted me to do: go to college, get a job, get married. Neither one of us would be in this mess now." I took a deep breath. "There's this big yellow house. Remember the surprise I told you about? That was it. Your house, that one you liked so much. I just wanted to see you retire and have somewhere nice. I'm sorry everything went so bad." And once the words were out of my mouth, I couldn't help the way I started crying. I heard sniffles behind me, and Jenson came and knelt beside me. She put an arm around my waist and rested her head against mine.

"It's not your fault, Jolene," she said, her voice thick with unshed tears. "You have to stop that."

I couldn't answer. My throat felt closed, tight, and if I opened my mouth I felt like I'd scream. There was another sniff behind us, and I heard Ryan telling someone to give us a minute. I glanced at Jenson and nodded. We stood up and walked toward the rows of chairs for people to sit in for the visitation. I caught Ryan's eye and nodded. He and David came back in, and Ryan strode up to me. His eyes were red and I realized, with a start, that he'd been the one I'd heard sniffling. It was so easy to forget about his hearing. Of course, he'd heard every word I'd said to Mama. There was relief in not being completely alone with it. My eyes met his, and he gave a small shake of his head, then bent and pulled me into his arms. I rested my forehead against his shoulder and tried to calm the sobs that still escaped every once in a while.

"You're okay. You're okay. You're tough, just like she was. Remember, you told me and David and Jenson all that stuff she went through, how she kicked ass every day to make sure you had food on the table. Remember that?" he said in my ear, low. I nodded. "You've got that same strength in you. And no matter what you think you are, she knew you, and she loved you. Don't let the rest of this shit make you forget that. Ever."

I stayed there for a moment, regaining my breath, trying to clam down, trying to tune out the voices of people coming into the room, the new round of sobs. After a few moments, I pulled back and looked up at Ryan.

"Thanks," I said shakily, and he nodded. Then he squeezed my hand. I heard someone say my name and I turned, recognizing one of the women who'd worked with Mama just as the rest of StrikeForce arrived, streaming in the door in their funeral clothes. I spent the next hour talking to people, listening to how sorry they were, what a good woman my Mama was and, more, person after person came up to me to tell me that she'd changed their life, that she'd been there at a crucial time and they don't know if they would have made it through certain things without her. And all I could do was nod, because yeah, that was Mama.

Jenson, David, and Ryan stayed near me the entire time.

Finally, it was time for the procession to the cemetery. Jenson left, as instructed, to pull her car into line. Ryan, David, two of my neighbors, and two men from Mama's work volunteered as pallbearers, and I watched numbly as they maneuvered the coffin from the funeral home and into the back of the hearse. When that was done, we got into our cars. We were right behind the hearse. I would rather not have been. I was grateful that Jenson was driving, and I could be in the back seat, not looking at the back of the hearse. Instead, I looked out the window. Ryan reached over and took my hand, and I twined my fingers with his. My three patrol partners had made sure they'd had my back in every way since all of this shit had happened, and I wasn't used to it. I didn't want to trust it. I mean, look at how well trusting people had worked for me so far. But they'd been there, through working together, to training me and helping me figure shit out, to now, when I was at my lowest.

"Guys," I said.

"Are you okay?" Jenson asked, looking at me in the rearview mirror.

"Okay enough. I just wanted to… thanks for everything the last couple of days," I said, feeling awkward. "It's meant a lot."

"You know I'm always here for you, Jolene," Jenson said. "And I know you'd have my back if I needed you."

"Same," David said, and Ryan nodded.

We drove the rest of the way in silence, and when we finally got there, the rain started up again. The ground was already waterlogged from the previous day's rain, and my heels sank into the soft earth as I watched the pallbearers bring Mama's coffin to the side of her grave. The marker wasn't there yet. The funeral home lady had told me it would be a few days.

I was glad the hole wasn't dug yet. This was symbolic, letting her loved ones and friends know where her grave would be when the time came. I din't want to think of her down there, which I knew was childish, but I couldn't help it. We stood there, and listened to a man from the chapel at the cemetery say a few words about my mother, and offer a prayer. Afterward, I watched as everyone walked past Mama's coffin, dropping a yellow rose onto it. As I watched. I got a prickle between my shoulder blades, as if I was being watched. I turned and looked around, but I didn't see anything. I turned my attention back to the coffin.

When there was only the rose in my hand left, and everyone was standing there, waiting for me, I finally forced myself to step forward and drop the rose onto the towering pile on the coffin.

"Love you, Mama," I whispered. "Bye." I went to stand with everyone else, and Jenson and Dani (whose eyes were red from her own mourning) put their arms around me as we watched the pallbearers load the coffin into the hearse one last time, and then we watched it drive away.

I barely made it through the wake. I thanked Jenson and her cousin, who had her same gray eyes, profusely for their help, and they both waved it away. I couldn't eat. All I kept thinking was that he'd pay. And it would start tonight. I was relieved when people finally started leaving and I could go home to Command. I needed to sleep, and then I had one more thing to do to honor Mama's memory.

# CHAPTER EIGHTEEN

When I woke up, I got up and scrubbed my face. My eyes were still red from crying, but now I felt numb. It was better that way.

I pulled my hair into a messy bun, blew my bangs out of my eyes. I pulled on a pair of black pants, my old black boots from my burgling days, a black tank top and a black shirt. I looked at myself in the mirror, meeting my eyes in my reflection. This could go badly. Really badly.

Or it could end up fucking up Connor and all of his plans. Maybe more.

I pulled a black balaclava I'd picked up. It covered everything except my eyes, and that was exactly what I wanted. I stuffed Dr. Death's phone in my pocket after unplugging it from its charger, then I grabbed the backpack with the stuff I'd bought from Lola inside and put it on my back.

I made my way quickly from my room up to the flight bay, doing my best to avoid cameras and our guards. I didn't want any attention or questions. I made it through, having timed their shift change pretty well, then took off into the sky.

I flew quickly, the night sky a blur as I focused on where I was going, on following the gps on my phone.

It took me less than two hours of flying to make it to the little island off the Mexican coast. I never would have guessed that I flew that fast. I circled around twice when I got over the facility I'd seen on the satellite maps David had showed me. I saw two armed guards at the gate, two more at the door to the facility. I pulled the x ray goggles David had been working on down over my eyes, noting thankfully that the building seemed to be empty. I landed near the gate, sending power blasts at both guards before they even realized what happened. I quickly tied them up and flew them to the dock, well away from the building. I made my way to the entrance of the building. I was able to knock one guard out by taking him by surprise, but he second guard started shooting at me immediately. I ducked and dodged his fire, then managed to get a blast in at him when he was trying to aim again. It knocked him back, but not out, and I ended up having to dive at him and knock his ass down. He fell back against the building and I heard his head crack against the brick wall.

"Don't be dead," I muttered, checking for a pulse. When I felt one, I sighed in relief, then tied both of those guards up and flew them to the docks.

It had taken me about two minutes, all together.

I pulled out the jammer I'd used so often to disrupt the alarm systems in the mansions I used to rob. I turned it on and smiled to myself. I hadn't planned on using this ever again. There was an alarm system, as well as a keypad type security system on the door. Within seconds, I had the security code cracked, and, about a minute later, the signal that the alarm system was compromised.

I made my way in, quietly opening the door. Inside, the lab was lit mostly with fluorescent lights hanging from the ceiling. Machines and other equipment I didn't recognize sat covered in dust. I swore under my breath, wondering if Death had been lying to me at the end about where he'd conducted his work. This place didn't look like anything but an old science junkyard.

There was a door to the left, and I went there. It was locked, but all it took was a good pull and the doorknob cracked in my hand. I swung the door open and saw that the office beyond was lined with binders, notebooks. Vials were collected neatly on racks, waiting to be used. Microscopes and other equipment were arrayed on countertops around the perimeter. I pulled one binder off of the shelf and looked it over quickly. I didn't understand most of it, but a few pages in, I started recognizing his notation for certain powers, notes about how he combined them. Several pages about how the formula wasn't stable, about how it had to be injected immediately, because storage produced irregular results. I put the binder back then rooted through the vials and other stuff in the cabinets. Not a drop of anything. On one wall of the office, I saw another door. I pushed it open and found that it led into a cooler. Along the walls, there was vial after vial of dark liquid, and I realized what I was looking at.

There were dozens of them. Labeled not with names, but with a number that, I guessed, matched up to the codes Death had kept in his binders. Dozens of vials of super powered blood, the precious samples that Connor wanted so badly that he'd apparently kill for them.

I nodded, dug one of the boxes I'd bought from Lola out of my bag, and attached it securely to the wall of the cooler with some putty adhesive she'd included with them. I powered it on, checked the signal button, and walked back out.

I went through the rest of the lab, which looked just as deserted as it had on first glance. All of the important shit, apparently, was in that one corner office.

I took the other two boxes out and did the same thing, placing one on the back wall and one just outside the office.

I walked outside, a good distance away from the building. I dug Dr. Death's phone out of my pocket and opened the video messaging app.

I dialed Connor and he answered after the first ring. His face came onto the screen, which I held pretty close to my own face. For now.

"Jolene," he said. The way he said my name had once made my body warm, my knees weak. Now all it did was make me want to flay him alive.

"Connor."

"I wondered where his phone went," he said after a moment. "Calling to tell me that you've come to your senses, sweetheart?"

I kept my face expressionless. "I'm not really in the mood for this right now," I said quietly.

"Of course. It was a nice funeral, though."

My stomach twisted, and I felt bile rising in my throat. That feeling of being watched earlier.... "You were there," I said.

"Of course. And you felt me. I saw when you turned around." He paused, his eyes glinting. "Don't you see it, sweetheart? How attuned we are? How much we belong together?"

"You never wanted me. You wanted my blood," I reminded him.

"Now we both know that's bullshit. I want you. I've wanted you since the second I laid eyes on you."

"You murdered my mother."

"Well, now. I gave you my reasons for that. What? Are you going to hold it against me forever? She's gone, and there's no changing it now." He looked into the screen, the cool light from his phone casting his face in harsh light, making his scar stand out even more. "And you still care, or you wouldn't have bothered calling me. We both know that."

"That's not why I called."

"No?"

I shook my head. "I'm on a little trip," I said. Then I pulled the phone back so he could see the building behind me. I saw the second he recognized it, and smiled behind my balaclava. "Recognize it?"

"Big deal. So you found Death's lab. It's on international soil. I know how you superhero teams work. Portia will go through all of the proper channels. She'll get the tribunal involved and they'll try to get a permit. Which will be denied, by the way, because I have servants in high places." He paused. "And if they do happen to get there, they'll find it empty. Do you think I'm stupid enough to leave that shit there? I have a crew en route now."

"I'm sure you do," I said.

"Go on. Try it. Get your search and seizure order and we'll see how that goes."

"Yeah." I shook my head. "I'm starting to think that you never really knew me at all, Connor."

His eyes narrowed. "Why's that?"

"Because if you did, you'd know I'm not that subtle." I pulled the remote out of my pocket and held it up so he could see it.

"Don't you fuckin' dare, Jolene. Don't even— "

I smiled, and then I hit the button. There was absolute silence for a moment, and then there was a deafening boom and all of the oxygen felt like it was sucked from of the air.

And then the lab burst into a ball of flame, and Connor started shouting on the phone. At first I couldn't hear him. Then I could.

"You fucking bitch. You'll pay for this. I swear to god I'll find you and — "

"I'm counting on it, asshole," I said. And then I hung up. I crushed the phone in my hand, turning it to nothing more than powder. I turned and took one last look at the inferno that had been his lab, and then I rose into the sky.

This didn't make us even. Not even close. It didn't avenge Mama. He still had his team and a hell of a lot of power.

But it set him back quite a bit, destroyed his little super army plan. And it ensured that this time, it was Connor having a bad day instead of me.

# CHAPTER NINTEEN

It was just after dawn when I got back to Command. The sky was a mix of aqua and coral in the east, a layer of vibrant yellow on the horizon that made me think of Mama, and I felt a little bit of the suffocating heaviness inside me lift. I landed in the flight bay to see Jenson already there, leaning against the wall.

I grimaced, readying myself for a lecture about protocol and international incidents and what could have happened if Connor had been there already. I walked toward her, and she watched me, expressionless. I reached her and was about to say something. I saw the corners of her mouth lift, just a little, and then she wordlessly raised her fist, and I bumped it with mine. Then she grinned.

"I should be pissed off, because I was worried sick about you. But you did it." She laughed. "I can't believe you did that."

"Portia's going to be pissed," I said, and we started walking toward the elevator.

"Portia is caught between being pissed that you did what you did and relieved that now she and StrikeForce don't have to get involved. I don't think you're going to hear much about it either way."

I glanced over at her, and she continued. "Portia's very by the book, but even she knows that sometimes you can't do things that way. As far as she's concerned, she doesn't know a damn thing about it," she explained.

"I don't think this is the last time she's going to have to turn a blind eye to what I'm doing."

"And I think she knows that. I think she doesn't want to hear about any of your plans regarding Killjoy, and the two of you will get along just fine. Those may have been her exact words, and she may or may not have told me to make sure I told you that."

I smiled. "Okay. Well. I have plenty to do still."

"We do."

"We, huh?"

"Yep. David and I were pretty good at helping you with the technical and intelligence-gathering stuff. Ryan did an amazing job training you to work with what you have, power wise, despite the fact that you didn't want to do it. I don't know where you got those devices, though."

"And you really, really don't want to."

"I really don't," she agreed. "Do you think he knows about it yet?"

I laughed. "Oh, he knows. I made him watch it happen. Called him via Death's phone."

She shook her head. And then she laughed. "Remind me never ever to piss you off."

"Just don't ever betray me, and we'll be fine," I said. We stepped on the elevator, and she pressed the button for our floor.

"Jolene."

"Hm?"

"I know you probably won't believe it, and I don't blame you, given what you've been through. But I wouldn't betray you. Ever."

I took a breath.

"You're going to play everything close to the chest now, waiting for the next person to turn on you. And I get it. I have been there." I looked up at Jenson, wondering again what her story was. I knew nothing about her past, other than the barest generalities. She was closed off about anything personal, which was why it had been so surprising that she'd had her cousin host the wake. As far as any of us had known, Jenson didn't have any family nearby. I didn't even know if Jenson was her actual name. All I knew was that when we all started calling one another by our real names, she'd still been Jenson.

"I trust you," I said. "Until I have reason not to."

She smiled. "Sounds fair. So what's next?"

"Next, I'm going to take a long shower, and then I'm going to sleep. A lot." I paused. "I need to clean out Mama's trailer at some point, but not now. I just can't deal with it right now."

Jenson nodded. "If you want help, you know all you have to do is ask."

"Thanks. I also need to pay for the last of the repairs on the house."

"Are you going to keep it?"

I shook my head. "I had an idea about that. Can we transfer the deed to StrikeForce? Like, make it look like Jolene Faraday donated it to the team? I mean, that's what I want to do, kind of."

"I don't think that would be too much trouble. I can get legal on it if you want."

I nodded.

"Why, though?"

"Remember Darla and her family?"

"Yeah?"

"They're dragging their feet about picking out a house for me to buy them. I think they feel weird accepting help. But what if StirkeForce just happened to have this house, specifically for this type of reason, where a super powered person needed it for a while? They couldn't possibly feel weird about using something that already exists for that purpose, right?"

She studied me. "I think that's a great idea. And a good way to honor your mother's memory. Her house will end up being a haven for people who need it."

"I thought she might like that. I just wish she could have lived there for a while."

We parted ways once I got to my room, and I let myself in and fell into bed. I could shower later.

I was in the workout room, blissfully alone. I'd had the early morning patrol shift, and then I'd come here, just as I had for the past five days since my face-off against Killjoy. The rest of my teammates seemed to understand that what I really needed right now was to be left alone, and, for the most part, they kept their distance.

Most of my spare moments, I spent in the training room.

I was still wearing my uniform; I hadn't bothered changing out of it after my shift. I stood in front of a heavy punching bag. It was black, hung from the ceiling with thick chains that clanked in a satisfying way when you hit the bag. I tried a couple of regular punches. Slow and pathetic, just as they'd been before. It was starting to become clear that I was never getting that part of myself back. And, honestly, it was the least important thing I'd lost, considering.

I could still hit hard, but I was so slow that unless the person didn't see it coming, I didn't have a chance in hell of actually hitting anyone.

I patted the bag, then stepped away, counting the steps it took to get me to the other side of the room. Twenty-seven. Twenty-seven steps took me to the edge of the sparring area. There were six concrete pillars spaced throughout the room, thirty-six recessed lights. Four weight machines; twenty-two sets of hand and free weights.

The counting is something I'd started doing the morning after Mama died. I'd listened to the heat kick on four times, counted the birds that flew by outside my bedroom window. I guess it was a way of coping, a way to keep from thinking about everything. I'd take it. It was stupid, but I'd take it.

Once I reached the other side of the room, I turned and looked back at the punching bag. It was easy to picture it as Killjoy (I refused to think of him as a person named Connor anymore), clad in black just as he always was. I took a breath, focused, and let loose an energy punch. It hit the bag with a satisfying "thump," and the bag shook, just a little, on its chains. I did it again, and again, and again, picturing Killjoy's death-black armor, hearing his voice in my head.

Again.

Again.

Again.

The bag started swinging wildly after each impact.

Again.

*So easy.*

*All I had to do was toss a few nice words and an ugly pair of socks I bought on clearance at Kmart in your direction.*

*Pathetic.*

I let out a loud growl and sent another energy punch. It impacted the bag, hard, and the chain holding the bag snapped. The bag went flying across the room, crashing into a weight bench and knocking it over before finally coming to rest.

"I'll tell Portia to order another one," I heard Jenson say behind me, and I turned to look at her. Her arms were crossed, and she was watching me. "Feel any better?"

"No."

She walked in and sat on one of the benches along the wall, crossed her legs.

"Nobody found Death's body," she said softly.

"So he might have made it," I said.

"Or his people grabbed the body when they disappeared, not knowing if he was alive or dead. You said

Killjoy stabbed him through the chest. I doubt he survived that."

I nodded. "I hope he didn't."

"Yeah." She started to say something, closed her mouth, then opened it again as if she was trying to figure out how to say something.

"What is it? Spit it out," I said, and she gave me a small smile.

"You know… if Death somehow had died at your hand, I wouldn't judge you badly for it," she finally said.

"You think I killed him?"

"I don't know. Chance was asking if maybe you'd actually done him in, and I said as far as anyone knew, it was Killjoy."

I took a deep breath. "I didn't kill him," I told her. "I wanted to. God, how I wanted to. When I first grabbed him in his apartment, I was so close to doing it, Jenson. But it wasn't me."

She nodded. "Okay. I figured that. And… when we finally come up against Killjoy again? Will you let him live?"

I met her eyes. "I can't make any promises there," I answered in a low voice.

"Fair enough," she said. Then she sighed. "Killjoy. I still can't believe it."

"That makes two of us," I said quietly.


The next day, I attended the small memorial service Portia had organized for Monica, Marie, and the rest of the people we'd lost when Killjoy's people had pulled their little jail break. Portia, being Portia, had insisted on keeping it light, on celebrating their lives instead of focusing on how they'd died. I watched Dani closely throughout. I had to give Portia credit: it seemed to be exactly what she'd needed. I hugged her at the end of the service, and Dani hugged me back hard, then pulled back and looked at me intensely.

"You hurt the son of a bitch, with what you did, didn't you?" she whispered.

'I did."

"You're going to hurt him more, aren't you?"

"Dani. I'm going to destroy the bastard. I promise."

She took a breath, and I saw some of the tension leave her shoulders. "Thank you. If there's ever anything you need, I'll do it. I want him and everyone working with him to pay for what they did."

"They will."

She nodded, and I hugged her again. As the service broke up, I headed out. I had to meet Justin at the house (I was trying to stop referring to it as Mama's house) to give him the last of the money I owed him for the repairs he'd done. They were finished now, and Jenson had gotten the StrikeForce legal department moving on transferring the deed. I took the bus, needing the extra time to think and be still.

There were about a million thoughts crowding my mind. Killjoy would lay low for a while and lick his wounds, but I didn't doubt that he'd come after me again, and probably sooner rather than later. Aside from that, there was the increase we were seeing in super human disappearances. Part of me wanted to think that was Killjoy, but kidnapping and imprisonment wasn't really his style. He just destroyed, then took what he wanted. There was also the issue Death had alluded to, about the formula being unstable and that being the cause of the low success rate of his tests. Killjoy was the only test subject to successfully integrate the formula into his body. What did that mean for him? I mean, hopefully it meant that eventually his body would painfully reject the formula, or it would wear off, or something like that. But I was getting used to the idea that things only get worse. I wasn't holding my breath waiting for him to just kind of fade away.

There was something still nagging me about the day Killjoy's people got into Command. They had

Damian/Virus, which made it easy for them to get doors open and things like that, because he just manipulated the circuits. But something struck me the day we had watched the security feeds from that day. The security cameras outside the building went off about five minutes before it happened, as did the ones at the main entrance, which was where they'd come in. There were no guards at the front entry, which is where we usually put our best people. They both said they'd responded to an alarm on the lower level. When I checked the video feed from that area to see what it was, I'd found that the cameras in that area were — surprise, surprise — also mysteriously not working.

So, yeah. Maybe Virus's powers somehow messed up only the cameras in three strategic positions. But they'd wanted to be seen. They wanted us to see how easy they did it. Christ, Maddoc had even waved and taunted me through one of the cameras.

It pointed to something I really didn't want to think about too closely, which was the possibility that one of our own had helped them get in so easily.

I closed my eyes and listened to the various sounds on the bus. The usual, quiet conversation, the faint, tinny sound of music coming from someone's headphones. When I opened my eyes again, I glanced down at my phone and noticed that there was a new message. Unknown number. I hit play and held it close to my ear.

"Bet you thought that was cute, huh Jolene?"

My stomach twisted. Because of course, it would be him.

"I said some things the other night that I didn't mean." I stared at my phone in disbelief. "I should have known better. Going after your mother was a terrible idea, sweetheart. I'm sorry." He was quiet, and I could hear him breathing. "I went too far. I lost sight of some things. You made me see that. Because I've lost you completely now, haven't I?"

Uh, obviously. "Jackass," I muttered, and the woman sitting a couple seats over looked at me. "Not you. Sorry," I said, and she nodded.

He was still talking. "I just don't think you understand what I was trying to do, Jolene. I'm not trying to destroy anything, or rule the world or any shit like that. I'm trying to save it. I'll make you see. I'll be seeing you around."

The message ended, and a chill went down my spine. He was really freaking delusional. I mean, just out of his goddamn mind.

And I hadn't seen it.

How do you miss something so obvious? And it wasn't just me. I knew that Ryan was dealing with his own frustration over not seeing Killjoy for what he was, for encouraging me to trust him. Maybe the formula had done something to him. I kind of wanted to believe that, just so I could think that maybe I wasn't really that blind. But the fact was that he'd been emailing Alpha about his plan before he'd even met me, and long before Death had come up with an even remotely successful injection to give anyone.

It struck me, then, that he might have left a trail of bodies in his wake. Not just Mama, and Death... but all the traveling he did. All those reports about him helping out in different areas of the world, being a "public hero" as he'd called it. I wondered now, what he was really doing there.

It was something to look into.

I wanted to delete his message, but I kept it. I kind of wanted Jenson to hear it. I don't know why. Maybe so I wasn't the only one having to hear how nuts he sounded.

The bus rolled up to my stop and I got off and walked the six blocks to the house. It was sunny, and warm for winter in Detroit. I had my hands stuffed into my jacket pockets, clenched tightly as I turned onto the block with the house I'd bought. I made it up the steps and onto the porch without falling apart, even though I kept picturing the porch swing I'd intended to buy for Mama, because I could just see her sitting and reading out there in summer. I pushed it away and let myself in. Justin's truck was parked in the street, so I knew he was already there.

"Hey, Jolene," he said when I walked in. He was wiping down the kitchen counter.

"You clean, too?" I joked, and he grinned.

"Not for everyone."

I nodded, and pulled the check I had for him out of my pocket. "Here's what I owe you."

He took it, searching out my eyes. I looked away.

"I hope your mom likes it," he said, and I took a deep breath.

"My mom passed away," I told him, forcing myself to look up. He stared at me in stunned silence, then recovered himself.

"I'm so sorry. Holy shit. What happened?"

I shook my head, blinking to keep myself from crying. He reached out and took my hand, and I gently pulled it away.

"Besides that... what happened last time..." I shrugged.

"Okay. I'm sorry. I shouldn't have done that. I didn't plan to."

"I know. And if it makes you feel better, it was a hell of a kiss. But I'm just not in the right place to even think about anything like that."

"Not even just being friends?"

I met his eyes. "You seriously wouldn't be wondering about kissing again? Or maybe more? Because I would be."

"You think men and women can't be friends?" he asked.

"I know they can. I have several male friends, who are just friends. But we both know that's not what's going on here and it's stupid and disrespectful to both of us to pretend otherwise. Right?"

He took a breath, then nodded. "You're right." Then he looked around. "I really am sorry to hear about your mom, though. I almost felt like I knew her from hearing you talk about her."

I nodded. "She would have loved this place. You did an amazing job."

"So, what now? Are you going to live here?"

I shook my head. "I can't. And I can't sell it, either. I'm donating it."

"Oh, really?"

"Yeah. My mom would have approved. So I donated it to StrikeForce."

He furrowed his brow. "To... StrikeForce? Really?"

I nodded. "They sometimes need houses, for those times when things get out of hand and people are unable to go back to their old houses for whatever reason."

"Uh huh," he said, with a kind of pained expression on his face.

"And my mom was a big fan of the team. She just loved them," I said quickly, because I really didn't want to hear him say anything bad about my teammates, and I had a feeling that that was where he was going. The team has no lack of haters, and I guess he was one of them.

Admittedly, we probably deserve at least some of the dislike. Losing record, lots of property damage. I understand. I just didn't feel like listening to it.

"Well, that's good. It'll make a nice home for someone," he said, and I was glad he let it drop. We walked out the front door, and he locked up and handed me the spare key he'd been using. "Um. You still have my number. If you ever want to talk, or get together or whatever, I hope you'll call."

I looked up at him and met his eyes. "Thanks. Take care, okay?"

"You too." He stayed there for a moment, his eyes locked with mine, and then he sort of seemed to shake himself and turned and walked down the stairs. I watched him get into his truck and drive down the street.

I skipped down the stairs. Ah, well. It never would have worked, even without me grieving over my mom and dealing with my psychotic super villain ex-whatever-he-was. He was too nice. Too normal.

And I have that whole "terrible judge of character" issue. So… yeah.

I ended up walking for a long time, bypassing several bus stops as I made my way back toward Command. I felt lighter, but also emptier. I had the feeling that as much as everything hurt now, I was still not quite over the shock of losing Mama. I wondered how long I could hold onto burning rage, because I wasn't especially looking forward to the crushing sadness phase of mourning.

# CHAPTER TWENTY

*Two Weeks Later*

I flew.

Detroit sprawled far below, like a crazy quilt of concrete and grass, a border of blue where the river cut the land, separating Detroit from Windsor.

I flew north, finding myself, eventually, over the neighborhood where our trailer was. The trailer park came into view, glimpses of the roofs of the trailers between the gray clouds below me. My eyes were drawn to the end of Perdition Lane, the little yellow and white trailer. There was a ratty old car in the driveway, but it was the wrong one. Not Mama's. Someone else lived there now. The world had moved on, but it felt like I never would.

I circled around twice, three times. There were thirteen trailers on Perdition Lane. Four roads intersected the trailer park. Three blocks down, there was a church with two steeples.

Goddamnit. Now even the counting was starting to stress me out.

I closed my eyes and flew. I let the air soothe me, let the silence of being hundreds of feet above everyone else numb me, just for a little while.

After a while, I ended up at the cemetery. Mama's grave with its newly-installed enormous limestone angel loomed below. I came in for a landing, and sat on the grass near her grave. I rested my chin on my knees, wrapped my arms around my legs. I never understood people who went to the cemetery to "visit" with loved ones. But I'd found myself coming a couple times per week since the day of the funeral, to sit here and talk. I guess I wanted to believe that Mama was somewhere where she could hear me, see me. That she wasn't really gone, because that was a little too much to handle. I had to believe in a heaven of some kind, for now, at least. It comforted me when nothing else could.

I had to believe she was looking down at me. So I came, and I talked. And, sometimes, I even felt a little better afterward.

"He killed you... at least part of why he killed you was because he believed you were what was keeping me 'good.' Because I was doing the hero thing, trying to make you proud." I paused, looking at her headstone without seeing it. "At first, I was a hero because they forced me to be. And then I played the hero because I thought it was a way to fool them into letting me out. Then, after Maddoc, I did it thinking you'd be proud, that maybe I could leave my old self in the past and you'd never find out about her. But, after a while..." I took a breath. "I started doing it for me. Which is probably selfish. I mean, I should want to be a hero for everyone else. To save them or some lofty shit like that. Sorry," I said automatically, as if she was even there to raise her eyebrows at me the way she usually did. "But I do it for me. Because it makes me feel alive and like something I'm doing matters. Even though we're so bad at it." I rested my chin on my knees again. "He thought that, now that you're gone, I wouldn't have any reason to try to be a hero. But he doesn't realize that by taking you away, he did the one thing StrikeForce never managed to do. He made me decide, fully, to do this hero thing. I'm probably not going to be the hero most people want me to be. But I think, if you happen to be looking down from where you are... I think you'll be proud."

I sat there for a long time, not seeing anything, my mind a million miles away. Memories, mostly. Mama teaching me how to ride a bike. Mama comforting me with a warm hug and my favorite chocolate ice cream after a rough day at school. Mama, telling me she was proud.

I heard a rustling sound behind me and turned around. Jenson, David, Ryan, and Dani were there, and Dani held up a brown paper bag. "Tonight, we drink in memory of your mom and those we've lost," she said. They came and sat with me, fanning out around Mama's grave. Dani passed me the bottle, and I took a gulp, passed it to Jenson.

"And tomorrow, I make the bastard pay," I said.

"We have your back, Jolene," Jenson said. "You get that, right?"

I nodded. "Yeah. I do."

"Seeing what they had planned... we were talking about some things," David said quietly.

"What things?"

"I think we all understand here that the things that need to be done to end this... they're not things we can do wearing official superhero costumes," Jenson said. "You proved that with the lab. If we want this over, if we want him stopped, for good, and if we want to save people without messing around asking the tribunal if it's okay first, sometimes it's just not possible to do it the way Portia wants to. And I know you're already thinking this, but I'm telling you that you're not alone."

"This is my fight," I said.

"It's all our fight. You're not the only one who lost people because of him," Dani said.

"You are superheroes. Keep being that."

"We will. But for once, we get to decide what that means," Ryan said. I met his eyes, and neither of us said anything for a few moments. "I choose this. I'll put on the StrikeForce uniform and do what this city needs me to do.

And other times, I'm fine with doing the things nice people don't want to think about any of us doing."

"We all know this is going to get worse before it gets better. StrikeForce needs to have a strong public image to reassure people that everything is okay. That they're safe. That's why it's important. That's why we all keep wearing the black and gray," David said. "But the fact is, no one will really be safe unless those behind this shit are taken care of. I think we all know he's somewhere licking his wounds. And I think we all know he's not done."

"And there are other issues too, which StrikeForce has been afraid or unable to touch, which I think will come back to bite us if we continue to ignore them," Jenson said.

"Such as?"

"Super powered people going missing. Including one that went missing when Killjoy and his people were fighting our team and infiltrating our base. Which suggests to me that the disappearances aren't him."

I nodded.

"You already knew about the missing heroes," she said quietly, a note of surprise in her voice.

"I wanted to believe it was him. Still could be," I said, and she shrugged.

"Maybe. But it's something that needs to be looked at, and nobody's doing it."

We sat in silence for a while. I hadn't planned on this. On having them with me for this, but even I had to admit that having David and Jenson's smarts and tech skills and Ryan's recon and sniper abilities would make it all a lot more straightforward. I didn't quite know how Dani's screaming powers fit into secret ops missions, but I also knew that I had no business turning her away, not when she'd lost a loved one as well. I nodded, slowly. Jenson took a swig from the bottle and handed it back to me, and I took another drink.

"We'll get him," Dani said.

I nodded, and the five of us passed the bottle and sat there late into the night. After everything that had happened, it made me a little queasy to think about putting my trust in anyone, and I didn't know if I'd fully be able to do so. I knew that Jenson, David, and Ryan had been with me through the worst, even if I didn't understand why. Dani was someone I'd once saved and we now shared a common enemy. For now, I'd see how it all played out, but I doubted I'd be able to fully trust them, and that was one more thing to hate Killjoy for.

But for now, they were here with me, and it meant a lot. It meant that I wasn't alone and I'd never realized before how much that could mean to me.

I looked back up at the angel over Mama's grave. Ryan bumped his shoulder against mine.

"You okay?" he asked softly.

"Not yet. But I will be."

It was all I knew how to be. If there was one thing I learned from my mother, from watching her support me on her own and keep us both clothed and fed, it was that you never let anything keep you down. You get up, and you make yourself do better. You don't stop fighting for those you love, not until you take your last breath.

I could wish all I wanted that I'd had just one more day, but in reality, that's something that isn't guaranteed for any of us. All we can do is make the most of what we have.

And what I have… all I have right now, is a hell of a lot of rage. That, and friends who are willing to face the darkness by my side.

It will have to be enough.

# EPILOGUE

"We need more hands on deck," Portia said as she and I stood at the end of the training center, looking over the couple dozen StrikeForce prospects who chatted or demonstrated their powers. "We had these people working here in other capacities. I think it's time to give a few of them promotions to full-fledged team members."

I looked around. "We can trust these people?"

She sighed. "About as much as we can trust anybody. We can't be picky at this point. I've worked with some of these people for almost ten years. They stuck with us through the craziness of taking control from Alpha, and several of them fought and were injured when Killjoy's people came to bust Maddoc and those guys out."

I guess it says a lot about my trust level that as I watched them, I was looking for those with the weakest powers to recommend for the team. That way if they did betray us, we wouldn't have too much of a fight on our hands. I shook my head, knowing I was being paranoid and that having a bunch of weaklings on our team wouldn't really help anybody.

"Well. Who's making the final choice again?"

"Jenson, David, and I," she said. "I asked Caine but he doesn't feel comfortable getting involved in the team management side of things. And you don't know any of these people," she added, as if she thought I might be offended that I hadn't been asked or something.

"Okay."

"It'll be okay," she assured me. "I'm thinking we'll bring two or three up to start with and once they're fully trained and we feel comfortable with them on the team, we'll look at promoting more."

I nodded, and we watched our prospective team mates for a while longer. We had some useful skills there, I had to admit. Several with enhanced speed, which was always handy. A couple of fire starters, one guy who could freeze things with his breath. A telekinetic, like Monica had been, I realized with a pang.

"We all know this is going to get worse," Portia said quietly as we looked at them. "You pissed him off now, and we actually kind of held our own against them when they attacked us. The tribunal is looking into not just our charges against Alpha, but also into your possible involvement in blowing up a lab in Mexico."

I took a deep breath, trying to keep myself calm.

She went on. "And the thing is, they have no goddamn proof of that, so I'm not too worried. Whoever did it was stealthy as hell about how they went about it. Kind of scary, really."

I smiled.

"The local media and that damn Detroit UnPowered guy are all over the fight between us and Killjoy. They're split on trying to decide if we were the heroes or the villains in that fight."

"Well. We'll train your new people. Suit them up in the gray and black, and we'll do better. Eventually they'll get their heads out of their asses and realize that we're the only ones who give a damn about this city."

She nodded. "Amen to that. All right. Let's get to it."

I left Portia to join up with Ryan for our patrol shift. I'd kept almost stupidly busy since Mama's funeral. I took extra patrol shifts when I could, monitored the detention wing fairly often because I just couldn't shake the idea that eventually, they'd have to come back for Alpha. His money had clearly been important to Killjoy, and Killjoy had some rebuilding to do. I watched as Jenson and Portia worked even harder to make StrikeForce's reputation stronger, watched David step up and do more public super hero stuff. I watched them all trying to convince the world that we could be trusted to keep them safe. And, in spare pockets of time, I met up with Dani, Jenson, David, and Ryan behind closed doors, trying to figure out the next non-official move we'd make to ensure that the promises StirkeForce made publicly would be upheld. And underneath it all, I burned with one overriding goal:

Revenge.

# The End

Jolene will return in *Darkest Day*,
the third book in the *StrikeForce* series
coming in March 2016.

# Never Miss an Update!

Sign Up for Colleen's Newsletter.
**http://bit.ly/colleensnewsletter**

For backstory material, news, and upcoming events be
sure to check out http://www.colleenvanderlinden.com

# LETTER FROM THE AUTHOR

Thank you so much for reading *One More Day*! I have been having so much fun with this series, and we're going to keep it going with book three, which will be out in March, 2016. I hope you'll come along for the ride and see what craziness happens in Jolene's life next. If you enjoyed this book, I would greatly appreciate your review on *Amazon*, and, of course, I always appreciate hearing from you via email (email@colleenvanderlinden.com), Twitter (c_vanderlinden), or Facebook (colleenvanderlinden). And if you want to keep up with my releases as well as read some of my stories before they're ever published, I hope you'll visit my website at www.colleenvanderlinden.com.

Writing a book is a very solitary pursuit, but publishing a book requires a team. I am lucky to have a phenomenal team helping me with these books. First of all is my husband and partner in crime, Roger, who is my designer, tech guy, website designer, therapist, and just all-around hero. I also worked with a brilliant team of beta readers on this book, and their input, without a doubt, improved this story. Thanks so much to Danielle Calleja, Susan Cambra, Jo Dawson, Krys Hopkins, Sarah Leenart, Jayna Longstreet, Sam McMullen-Hamilton, Kari Powers, Rachel Scott, and Samantha Wheeler. You guys are the best.

As always, my wonderful family deserves an award just for putting up with me sometimes. I love you guys.

Huge thanks to everyone who buys my books or checks them out via *Kindle Unlimited*. Thank you for your support, which allows me to keep writing and publishing these crazy stories of mine.

Colleen Vanderlinden
Detroit, Michigan
January 18, 2016

# ABOUT THE AUTHOR

Colleen Vanderlinden is the author of the *StrikeForce* series. She is also the author of the *Hidden* and *Soulhunter* urban fantasy series', as well as the *Copper Falls* paranormal romance series. The third *Hidden* novel, *Home*, was a finalist for *RT Book Reviews' Editors Choice Awards* for best self-published urban fantasy novel of 2014.

Her books have consistently received positive reviews, and *RT Book Reviews* has called her storytelling "electrifying."

She lives in the Detroit area with her husband, kids, demonic Basset hound, and two lazy cats. You can find out more about Colleen's books at her website, colleenvanderlinden.com, or follow her on Twitter, where she's @C_Vanderlinden.

## The StrikeForce Series
A New Day
One More Day
Darkest Day – *Coming March 2016*

## The Hidden Series
Book One: Lost Girl
Book Two: Broken
Book Three: Home
Book Four: Strife
Book Five: Nether
**Hidden Series Novellas**
Forever Night
Earth Bound

## The Hidden: Soulhunter Series
Guardian
Betrayer

## The Copper Falls Series
Shadow Witch Rising
Shadow Swor

## Never Miss an Update!
Sign Up for Colleen's Newsletter
**http://bit.ly/colleensnewsletter**

CPSIA information can be obtained
at www.ICGtesting.com
Printed in the USA
LVOW04s1827080416
482783LV00013B/91/P

M0334 2254